# Seeing People Off

*A*
*Novel*

## Jana Beňová

Translated by Janet Livingstone

*Two Dollar Radio*
*Books too loud to ignore*

# Two Dollar Radio
## Books too loud to Ignore

**WHO WE ARE** TWO DOLLAR RADIO is a family-run outfit dedicated to reaffirming the cultural and artistic spirit of the publishing industry. We aim to do this by presenting bold works of literary merit, each book, individually and collectively, providing a sonic progression that we believe to be too loud to ignore.

**TWODOLLARRADIO.com**

Proudly based in
**Columbus**
**OHIO**

@TwoDollarRadio

@TwoDollarRadio

/TwoDollarRadio

**Love the PLANET?**
So do we.

Printed on Rolland Enviro, which contains 100% post-consumer fiber, is ECOLOGO, Processed Chlorine Free, Ancient Forest Friendly and FSC® certified and is manufactured using renewable biogas energy.

PERMANENT    100%    BIO GAS ENERGY    Ancient Forest Friendly™

*Printed in Canada*

**SOME RECOMMENDED LOCATIONS FOR READING *SEEING PEOPLE OFF*:**
Elevated places—tops of hills, vineyards. Cafés and wine bars with high spirits.
Double-decker buses, planes, hot air balloons, and trees.
Or, pretty much anywhere because books are portable and the perfect technology!

**AUTHOR PHOTOGRAPH→**
by Vladimir Simicek

**COVER DESIGN→**
by Two Dollar Radio

THIS BOOK HAS RECEIVED A SUBSIDY FROM SLOLIA Committee,
the Centre for Information on Literature in Bratislava, Slovakia.

# Seeing People Off

## A Manifest of the Quartet

# I
## PETRŽALKA
### The Galapagos

## PETRŽALKA
### The Shadow of My Smile

## PETRŽALKA
### My Own Style

## PETRŽALKA
### The Sound of My Heart

## PETRŽALKA
### Always on My Mind

The neighbor living next to Ian and Elza is an older man. For years he's been thinking that Elza is Ian's son. He greets her genially with "Hi there," or sometimes a friendly thump on the chest.

The neighbor can't stand firecrackers. When the children start setting them off, he runs out onto the balcony and yells:

"You motherfucker!" Over and over again. This is how the new year begins in Petržalka. *Youmotherfuckeryoumotherfuckeryou!*

The neighbor's not a person—he's basically a peculiar firecracker. A bullet. The next night, Elza makes a pilgrimage to his door so that she doesn't have to listen to TV shows through his wall. She asks him to turn it down. His eyes are shining: a combination of alcohol and tears.

"I'm not sure," he says aloofly, full of positive energy. "It's a program to support the Tatra Mountains, so I thought everyone, everybody..." whimpers the neighbor.

Elza leaves, enters her apartment, the television isn't blaring through the wall anymore. Now the neighbor is blaring: "Hungarian whores!" Over and over. Elza is lying in bed, tears rolling down her face. Over and over. To support Petržalka.


Petržalka is a place where time plays no role. There are creatures here that the rest of the planet thinks are extinct, died out. Good and bad. The faces of cockroaches remind us of dinosaurs, and the neighbor's voice doesn't come from his throat, but from the eye teeth of a wildcat.

Elza runs out onto the balcony, takes a bottle from the waste basket, and leans over onto the neighbor's side. By the wall stands an empty aquarium. She throws the bottle into the middle of it, runs back in, and hides in bed. She hears the neighbor go outside, and it's quiet for a moment. Elza is shaking.

"Pinot noir," reads the surprised neighbor from the shards after a moment. Then peace settles over the land.


In Petržalka apartments, all the walls play music and talk. You'll be reminded here of songs you thought the world had long forgotten. Time stands still. Radios are tuned to the same station for years. The needle showing the stations has sunken into the bowels of the machine. To the bottom of the theme park. Elza found out that they still play the show *Birthday Music*. She remembered it from childhood. During socialism they played it in every hair salon.

Elza asks the neighbor not to listen to songs and birthday wishes so loud. The neighbor stands in the doorway in his underwear, barefoot. Weeping. While listening to the brass band, he was reminded of his dead mother.


His two sons visit him: "Get a hold of yourself, Dad! You're losing it! What's wrong with you? You call me on the Czech mobile network when I'm in Austria! I pay for all that. Look at yourself! Jeez! Get a hold of yourself! I tell you something and two weeks later you've forgotten."

"Don't talk to me about details! I don't want details," the father beseeches.

Elza decides to wait in the street outside their house to catch them and ask them not to broadcast their family affairs so loudly until three in the morning. After standing in front of the entrance half the day, she finds that she can't tell the neighbor's sons from other young Petržalka men. They're all tall and beefy with shaved heads, and their faces look like pancakes.


**Elza.** In my childhood, the land on the other side of the river seemed dangerous. My parents and I lived in the Old Town. The Old Bridge is the beginning of an unpredictable road— the walkway on the left side is suspended over an abyss with a brown river rushing below. This is the border, where a Sunday stroll changes to a fight for one's life. That's why only adults over eighteen should walk along it.

From the city side of the river I often look at the Luna Park— the gateway to Petržalka. I try to avoid the scorching eyes of the sphinx. They guard the entrance while feigning playfulness. Horses, ducks, and swans of monstrous proportions and colors turn in a closed, airtight circle. Twirling in a devilishly defined track. Above them, jumping, screaming children whirl around. The relentless turning movement absorbs the landscape.

There's no escape—the circle can't be breached. A few children have chosen badly—now they're clutching the necks of the plastic horses and crying.

"This is what I call life," says the man running the merry-go-round, and lifting his face to the sky, he turns up the speed.

Some days the Luna Park looks like it's closed and broken. Only a couple of merry-go-rounds and a shooting range are operating. The guys who run it wander around the muddy complex. Their tragic figures remind me of England in times when they used children as chimney sweeps.

Driving a blue car in the bumper car arena, I crash into a red one and get the wind knocked out of me. Whenever the subject of merry-go-rounds arises, my father always talks about the swan that came off while two little kids were on it.

My grandmother accompanies me into the hall of mirrors and when we can't get out—no way, no doors, the mirrors aren't windows, nothing, just me and Grandma, Grandma and I, and our faces in the mirrors getting paler and paler—after a half hour we begin to yell for the man who sold us the tickets to lead us out. To show us the way.

A few years later Mama and Grandma get lost in Petržalka. They get on the right bus, but going the wrong way. Instead of downtown, it ferries them deeper and deeper into the high-rise housing blocks.

When they get off, terrified, it's already dark and snowing. They'll never get home, never find their way out. "Miss! Miss! Excuse me, how can we get to Bratislava?" Mama blurts to a young woman at the stop. "But you already are… You are in Bratislava," says the woman, surprised.

Mama smiles helplessly. "I mean to the city. To the city of Bratislava!" When they finally get across the bridge, Mama asks Grandma if she noticed what an odd face that girl had. Like a pancake.

When Ian and I want to make love for the first time, he tells me that he lives in Petržalka. I don't even shudder. (I realize that I still haven't shuddered.)

The bridge is dangerous, especially if you cross it on foot. The river is too close. The boundary between the water and the air calls you. I'm afraid I'll just suddenly jump. Without warning, without one sad thought, without saying *shoop*, no drama or decisions—regular steps along the bridge will just be replaced by a jump.

The strongest urge to jump I have in winter. In those layers of warm clothes, a person feels impenetrable and inviolable. And longs for a change. Like a nomad longing for a change of scene—in winter I long for a change of state. Instead of unsure, sluggish steps along the icy surface of the bridge, a jump would be flight. Then the moment of transition. Prolonged for a little while when I'm already lying in the water but it hasn't yet soaked through the layers of clothing to my body. It gets through slowly, heavy, green like a menthol candy—it fills the pockets, gets into the shoes.

The pancake got on the bus. He shoved his fat tattooed shoulder in my face. I closed my eyes. So I wouldn't have to look at those figures writhing in flames, or the pancake's face framed by a moonlit landscape outside the window. I let myself be driven and jostled with closed eyes.

Perhaps it was because of these Petržalka scenes that Ian went blind for a time a few years ago. He decided it was better to see nothing, not look around, not watch, not have to observe—Petržalka.

Ian remembered how once, after years, a childhood friend who had emigrated to Canada in '68 came to visit. He stared out the window of the Petržalka apartment for a while and never returned to his birthplace. "So this is how you live now," he said. He clapped Ian on the shoulder and left for home without a trace. He never called again. Petržalka had taken his Canadian breath away.

I've never liked tattooed people. They remind me of criminals and pirate ships. And a drunken worker on the summer tram. Mama and I were riding home from the swimming pool. "What are you lookin' at?" a worker boomed at Mama. He had a mermaid, a heart with an arrow through it, and the word 'Carmen' tattooed on his arm. "I'm not looking at you," said Mama and we moved to another section of the tram.

Sometimes I think that Ian didn't go blind for Petržalka. Maybe it was for me. He couldn't stand to look at our life anymore. Like looking at a tattoo. He went to the other part of the tram.

And his Canadian friend never came back to Slovakia because he realized that he couldn't save anyone from Petržalka. Not even his first friend and former commander of their child army.

After Ian got his sight back, he hated things that reminded him of blindness. Slippery stones at the bottom of rivers, lakes, and the sea; mud; the films *Dancer in the Dark* and *Ray*; swimming goggles; and dark-colored groceries (beef, Chinese mushrooms, turkey legs).

He could only see out of one eye, though.

The pancakes are worshipers of the cult of death. Bald skulls are a sign of necrophilia. They hate everything that seeks the light, that sprouts, springs forth, breaks out of its shell. They are impressed by a naked, shining bone, a skull, pure calcium. Pancakes' hair gets a chance to grow only when they're already six feet under. Then, for the first time, it timidly sprouts from their skulls like feathers.

"Aha! Look, what's this?" shouts a little boy on the terrace in Petržalka and waves his arms in the air like a bird.

"Nothing," his friend answers.

"It's called *Heil Hitler*," says the boy and continues to wave his arms.

He takes off a bit.

Elza and Ian were Bratislava desperadoes. They didn't work for an advertising agency and weren't trying to save for a better apartment or car. They sat around in posh cafés. They ate, drank, and smoked away all the money they earned. Like students. (Slogan: *only genuinely wasted money is money truly saved*) They joined that carefree class of people who buy only what they can pee, poop, and blow out—recycle in 24 hours.

It was because of those desperate people that the cafés and restaurants in the city, where everything costs a hundred times more than it should, could stay open.

Once in a while, they would happily enjoy living in other places—in B&Bs or hotels. It didn't matter which city. It was a pleasure to live somewhere other than Petržalka. When they came home from traveling, they were always afraid to open the apartment door again. What could be waiting for them on the other side?

**Elza.** Some people get the runs when they go to Egypt. We always got it when we came home. To Petržalka.

Elza and Ian were making love. The voices of child führers playing their games in front of the building wafted in. Shouts. Cursing. It was autumn. Almost dark. The pleasure of man and woman mixed with the vulgarity of the children's shouting. They made love quietly and modestly. Gazing into each other's eyes. Like Jews hiding in a cellar.

Every famous city has views. You look out and suddenly it's lying at your feet, you see it as if in the palm of your hand, everything squeezed together. At some panorama points there are cafés where you can buy the most expensive bottled water and wine in the city.

At every lookout point there's an old man. Usually with white hair. He stands stealthily in the corner watching those who come to look. He has them in the palm of his hand, everyone squeezed together.

He approaches the defenseless ones, looks into their faces for a moment, and quickly his hands fly into the air as he begins to fire off names of well-known structures and monuments. He points from building to building, as if he were playing chess with the city and subtly moving them around. He continues despite your signaling that you know the city well. All the buildings and monuments too. That you're not a tourist. That you were born there and you only leave the city during the hot summer months.

Then he holds out his hand and asks for three euros for coffee.


**Elza.** I'm the Bratislava old man. I wait up on the castle hill. Here you get the best view of the tourists. I look around and choose. Then I approach my victims, look them in the face for a moment, stretch my arm out far in the direction of the other bank and point to the white city beyond the river: Petržalka, Petr-žal-ka.


As if I were an exact copy of old white-haired Freud at the moment the Gestapo summoned him. They moved in directly opposite his apartment, Berggasse 19. Their windows looked into his. Before they let him leave the country, he had to sign a paper saying that they hadn't done him any harm. The old man signed and added a sentence. "I can only recommend the Gestapo."


Voices were approaching. They thudded from the other side of the wall, came down from above, throbbed in the soles of our feet. The rhythmic singing of the Petržalka muezzins. They woke Elza up early in the morning. Before dawn.

In the apartment below lived an old woman with her invalid mother. They were always home and both were nearly deaf. Their never-ending conversation started before sunrise. They woke up early, couldn't sleep. Every morning the two old ladies examined existence—theirs and that of other people. From the beginning. They clung to their gossiping as if to life itself.

Elza lay in bed. The voices rising up from the apartment below disturbed her. She felt like the old women were croaking right inside the pillow under her head. They were there every morning. Since forever. Their old-woman household pulsed under her head.

"Mama, you are a really grumpy patient," screeched one old lady at the other.

"You're always nervous. You complain—about the doctors, nurses, the dialysis. You're horribly dissatisfied all the time. And in that room too—the other grandmothers just lie there quietly, not saying a word…"

"Because they're stupid," quacked the second old lady back. And as the sun rose, others joined in.


I can only recommend Petržalka.


The shrieks of a girl brought up on porn films, who screamed while she was fucking as if they were slicing her open. From the apartment to the left the monologue of a disappointed woman. "You got me drunk and then you secretly sold my antique watch, vultures. But this apartment is my property. I'll kick your asses. Get out of here, bastards. They keep everything from me, steal towels, bang up the pots. The main issue is that none of their stuff is damaged!"

The apartment was filled with loud music. Piercingly loud. The furniture and Elza shook. Someone ran out onto the balcony: "That's it! Do you hear me? The two of us are done! I loved you very much, but you've really offended me this time. But this time you don't have to deal with it anymore. I love you, but I don't need your involvement anymore. And it shouldn't matter to you at all how many dicksinmycunt!"

Elza ran out of the apartment and thought she would never come back. Home!

She walked around town for eternity, making loops around the posh neighborhood. Looking into lit-up windows. The streets echoed with the sound of her own muted steps. The silence radiated. Her breathing was deep and regular.

As soon as she crossed the threshold of her own apartment, it involuntarily quickened. Her belly was bloated with a mountain of muddy, slippery stones. It was quiet in the room. She waited. Like a deer in headlights. Like a rabbit ready to bolt.

The muezzins reminded her of bats. Blind mice with wings always making noises. They find their way, set their azimuth, their position, know where they are by how their voices ricochet off things around them. They orient themselves in the world by how their voices bounce off things, beings and landscapes around them. They give off sounds, looking for their place. They are amplified beings following the echo. Like people forever babbling into telephones glued to their cheeks. Quickly and continually blabbing, listening to the echo of their own yacking. They're looking for where they've gotten to. Where they've settled in the net.

Like blind people afraid of the dark who sing quietly to themselves. Like people who live alone in dark apartments and turn on the television first thing in the morning just to give the place some life.

Like a rapsodist who constantly tells the same stories over and over again. Stories that force themselves to be constantly told. Improved. So that they don't lose their place. So they have something to bounce off of. So the thread isn't broken.

**Elza.** Voices are so bewitching. They bore into the body. Gradually uncover all the paths. Some of them shut the gates forever, burn bridges. Close openings.

"What kind of fucked-up country is this?" yells the neighbor and laughs like a lunatic. I sit on the toilet and try to pee. The neighbor is laughing and yelling. His voice encircles me like a strap that's too tight. Like a harness. It digs into my flesh. As long as I have to listen to him, I can't pee.

The neighbor is an emphasized character.

You can't hear the Petržalka muezzins in the city. The river stands in their path. It doesn't carry their shouts. It swallows their calling with its own silence. Silence without competition.

The muezzins are powerless under the surface. The water swallows their words, stories, shouts. The earthly noise, meaning, and intensity. They back up from her. A few steps back—home—to Petržalka. Retreat like rats.

A city with a river running through it has an advantage over one without a river. It doesn't have to be exterminated all at once. A city without a river has to be exterminated all in one day. So that the rats don't get out of the poison zone into places that haven't been treated yet. A city with a river running through it can be poisoned in two steps.

When Elza left the apartment in the morning, Ian was sitting naked in a chair, writing. In the evening when she returned, she opened the door to the living room and was surprised to see him still sitting there naked, writing, in the same position. When she points it out to him, he slaps his belly and thighs with joy as if he were seeing them for the first time. He likes the lively sound of it.


That spring Elza and Ian started living in their city as if on vacation. Like being abroad. Reading for hours at Café Hyena. They listened to and watched the people around them. Maintained a state of wakeful hunger. Spent lots of money. As always, on the edge of being broke. Pissing it away. Always writing something.

They met at the café twice a day and shared the table with another couple—Rebeka and Lukas Elfman. It was obvious that this was a Quartet of artists. Rebeka was Elza's friend from childhood, and Elfman had married her just before it ended.

At the Hyena they were on a stipend. That's when life slows down to the pace of a ship cruise.

# II
## Café Hyena

"Oh little fairy, if you only knew what I've been through…"
—Pinocchio

**Elza.** Rebeka and I always met just before lunch. We would go shopping together and then we took our time drinking a bottle of red wine. Meanwhile, Rebeka would cook because, unlike me, she didn't like sandwiches, but preferred meat and sauces. All the honest, completely homemade meals, like Szegedin goulash or chicken and rice with compote moved her and reminded her of her family and eating with her mama, who had died.

Rebeka also liked to cook because wine went down well during cooking. "This is the way we live, Elza, cooking, cleaning, and drinking. Jeez, but sometimes I say to myself—we do it instead of working—but imagine those women who are at work till four and then they manage to do everything that's taken us all day." Rebeka lit another cigarette, took a deep drag, and for a moment quietly admired women who work. Rebeka was my best friend. We even looked like each other. There were days when people thought we were sisters. Rebeka didn't mind it. She also had one real sister—a twin. Their relationship got sticky when the sister went around in public yelling that, in their mother's womb, Rebeka had taken all the nourishment for herself.

Rebeka reproached her for not remembering anymore who saved her from being beaten up. "She was always baiting somebody, but didn't know how to defend herself afterwards. We were strange twins: we won all the competitions. I was always faster at running, swimming, and climbing. My sister always won the other battles, like who could eat the most pancakes or swallow a whole muffin."

Lately something had been bothering Rebeka. She was the only member of our Quartet who'd never worked. The ones with stipends met daily in the café so they could set the strategy. They had a system where one of them would always work and earn money while the others created. They sat around in the café, strolled around the city, studied, observed, fought for their lives.

The fourth, meanwhile, provided the stipend. Just as other artists get them from: the Santa Maddalena Foundation in Tuscany, the Instituto Calouste Gulbenkian in Lisbon, the Fulbright Foundation in the USA, or the Countess Thurn-Taxis in Duino.

The Trinity Foundation had its headquarters at the Café Hyena, which the patrons renamed Café Vienna. It was a spacious café patronized mostly by foreigners and rich people. Here they considered the Trinity to be students. They were always shivering with cold, not dressed heavily enough, warming their hands on the hot mugs, mixing all kinds of alcohol, and continually writing something or making notes in books or magazines. Sometimes they would close a book loudly, put their hand on its spine, and look off into the distance with a sigh. So the other guests knew that they had just gotten to an idea in the text that had suddenly completely changed their life. Sometimes they stood up and nervously walked around the café. Tapping their fingers impatiently on their lips. Creativity broadcast live.

Today at the Hyena, Elza is reading aloud from *Seeing People Off.* The first ten pages. The air grows tense from the vulgar words and a pair of older women and two families with children rise from a table covered with desserts and leave. At the end, no one applauds. A lady in violet comes over to Elza. "I don't easily go up to people and give them my opinion, but I have to tell you that Petržalka isn't like that. I don't know where you live—there are weirdoes everywhere, but this? Not like that! And I guarantee you that if you leave the beginning like that no one will buy your book. I guarantee you. And I'm not even a teacher."

When the Quartet discussed something, its members shouted over each other, rising out of their chairs with faces burning. Sometimes they celebrated here. On pay day, when the stipend came for the next month. Then they inordinately drank, ate, and argued. They filled the whole café with their yelling.

"Don't talk shit to me!" shouted Rebeka at Elza. They were arguing about the character of Cowboy in the Lynch film *Mulholland Drive.* For Elza it was a negative character and for Rebeka positive. He reminded Elza of a secret police agent, Rebeka of an alchemist. During their argument, Elza's friend's face changed from its original Rebeka-the-little-sheep, Rebeka-the-lamb, from doe-eyed-dog-Rebeka to Rebeka-the-wolf, -lion, -tiger, -dragon, and finally it glowed pure, blinding, motionless gold. And golden-mouthed-Rebeka shouted: "So shut your trap for a second, for God's sake, shut up, Elza!"

"You're not arguing with me, you're arguing with the wine," Elza laughed.

"I think it's time. She should start earning," said Elfman.

"Her? She's so frail," doubted Elza.

"Oh please, don't talk to me like some bisexual," said Ian, annoyed.

**Rebeka.** Money—again we need money. We can't live forever like this: with no money. Now it's my turn—I'll try to start earning. And we'll see. I'll find a job, start a business, I'll go to work, earn money, money, money, I'll be an employee, I'll settle in, fit in, straighten out my life, mature, become independent, secure.

I can do anything except teach. Teachers have it the worst. Even when they aren't at school, they hear a classroom full of kids everywhere: voices, chairs scraping, pencil case zippers, a compass being stabbed into someone's back.

In the deserted woods, the voices of children on a school trip come to them. They move with them, melding with the burbling of the brook. "Why did they take the kids on a trip to such a deep deserted forest? And why now, at midnight, on New Year's Eve?" the teachers ask themselves in the desolate wood. "And if we're asking this, then what for God's sake are the children asking themselves?"

Rebeka's grandmother was a teacher once. She talked about some of her students. For example, about a boy who called everyone a *loser*. His father was a musician who played Dixieland and the kids made fun of him, saying that he played dicksilant. Or about a woodworking teacher who cut off his finger during class and the kids saw him off to the hospital, laughing all the way. He carried his finger in a bucket full of ice. The doctors in the hospital poured it down the toilet and flushed.

Elza took care of the stipends for the Trinity last time. She worked under various pseudonyms in several competing daily newspapers. They were usually influential papers with national coverage and a common management center.

The first place she worked was in television. Under the pseudonym Kaufman, she was public relations manager for a reality show, which took place in the Dachau concentration camp. The blue group lived like imprisoned Jews, and the red group played the role of guards. There were great hopes for the show, especially financial.

The office reminded her of a scouts' camp or a kids' school classroom. The people, who worked crowded one on top of the other, ate at their desks, cursed, worked, and commented out loud on everything they were doing. They ran around and played their games.

At work, some tried to attach themselves to others. They looked for protection. Like those lonely beings who cried during the whole time at camp, missing their parents. "I'm never leaving home again," they said to themselves. And they gathered in pathetic, tight groups. A couple of children crying in their own little circle. The thing that had annoyed her most was the evening sessions where everyone sat around the fire and sang. One song after the other.

Little Elza always sat hidden in the back row, but just in case, she opened her mouth as if she were singing. She didn't make a sound. But from her moving lips you could read: "We are the children of a freeeee country."

She did the same now—at work. She moved her lips.


Around her, workers ran about hectically. They cursed, quickly catching their breath, were always behind, hissed and sizzled.

They didn't sleep, didn't eat. They didn't eat, didn't sleep—just whistled while they worked. They were heroes—neurotics running in circles. Their charm lay in their eternal dissatisfaction. ("God, why can't they let me finish one thing? Not now, I can't. I don't have time. I have work to do, I have to make myself a cappuccino!")

All the women at work called each other by the nickname "hon" and white poisonous spit collected in the corners of their mouths.

Red dots shown in the corner of every eye. Sometimes they switched languages. To a special women's language, Láadan. After *elasháana* and *husháana, osháana*—a word for menstruation—and *ásháana*, meaning to menstruate joyfully, were the next words which were supposed to guarantee women in Slovakia equality of rights.[1]


The concentration camp reality show was such a failure that it bankrupted the TV station. The whole network.

At a meeting, Elza's supervisor shouted that the problem was that viewers weren't engaged enough. "The war ended a long time ago, today we can't get any more mileage out of it."

"Unless we unleashed the war again," commented one of the special effects guys. The director threw that idea out. He used the argument that everyone would lose money if they did that. "During wartime, money loses value, the world operates on rationing coupons."

---

1   Láadan is a language created in 1982 by Suzette Haden Elgin intended to better express women, whose viewpoints were felt to be shortchanged in many Western languages compared with those of men.

---

In January, days came when Elza felt like her inner organs had disappeared from her body. Her breathing tubes ended just below the neck. Then she ate and drank. And she was surprised that those pieces of bread, tomatoes, and cookies disappearing into her mouth didn't immediately show up under her feet. Her breathing was shallow. It moved between her nose and mouth. Forget about asanas!

She remembered her grandfather's joke about Jánošík[2]. They hung Jánošík up by his rib, but he just kept hanging and wouldn't die. He asked the petty officer if he could have a cigarette. The officer said, okay, if it's your last wish... Jánošík went to the corner store for cigarettes and had a smoke. But the smoke came out of his lungs through the hole under his rib. He didn't get that true pleasure from smoking. He gave up, tapped the ashes from the butt, and jumped back up onto the hook.


Youth camp for some people started again in old age. Elza's aunt lived in an old age home in Budapest. On Margaret Island. Elza and her mother visited her once a month. She always wore gloves and smelled of old furniture.

In January, the old woman (gloves and all) jumped out the window. She committed suicide because she couldn't be in the bathroom for as long as she would have liked. She couldn't spend as long in the shower or in front of the mirror as she needed. There were always other people waiting at the door. Someone was always breathing down her neck. Knocking.

The old age home was a continuation of youth camp. A common bathroom, too much singing, scheduled meals that someone else chose for you, here and there a party.

---

2   Jánošík is a character from a Slovak legend similar to Robin Hood.

On the road home from Budapest a truck blocked their view the whole way. On the back it had a sign for Italy framed by tomatoes and bottles of wine. Elza thought of the sea, Pompeii, and Lagrima Christi wine. She longed for big cities—Lisbon, Rome, Amsterdam, and London. She associated them with a feeling of freedom and abundance.

In a foreign city, she and Ian always made love twice. In the morning and before going to sleep. They formed a pair that had to continually affirm itself—convince itself of its own homogeneity. Its functionality. It grew two new heads with clean tongues. They used them to lick the new country.

No one understood them, their speech became secret and romantic. They thought it up just for themselves. No one ruined it for them or expanded the borders of their world with seeming comprehensibility.

World events ceased to exist. Holding their breath, they scanned the headlines of the local newspaper, which they didn't understand. To Elza, foreign cities felt free because she had never worked there. She didn't know the mayors, the city neighborhoods, the offices, the scandals. She didn't have to chase anyone down in them, or call around. She had no contacts.


**Elza.** Bratislava. A city that grips you in its clutches. On the way from work to Ian and from Ian to work. Tied up in the rhythm of your own steps. The rhythm of the city. The rhythm of lovemaking, work, parties, earning and spending, gaining and losing. Are you making money? Combining ingredients? Time, men, and money? City, wine, song, and work? Friends, love, and idiots. Pancakes! The Bratislava alchemist.

Bratislava. A city that forces you to pounce on something, just as it has pounced on you.

In the newsroom. "What do you actually do, Elza, in reality? Are you writing a novel? Aha... You're lucky, I would do the same. If I had the time. If only you knew what I've been through. What a book that would be!" The Editor-in-Chief sighed and poured himself some white wine. *Oh, little fairy, if only you knew what I've been through...* He sat down on her desk, put his hands on his hips, and looked into her eyes.

"How are you doing—have you found anything out?"

"You know, I really don't know now, what's going on. What's true in this case. I don't have a way to confirm, but I'm trying— I'm calling around, asking, waiting."

Under her boss's blue-eyed gaze, Elza was flooded with heat. A blue flame burned directly in her face. She thought she could hold on and kept talking. But at one point she felt that if she didn't take off her turtleneck, she would burn up, explode, melt on the surface.

"At the beginning it seemed clear. But confusing information keeps coming in. We shouldn't panic," she continued, trying to pull her turtleneck over her head. She thought she could do it in one fell swoop. But her sweater got stuck just above her head and she was wedged inside it. "I'm not sure I'm going to make it by the deadline. But tomorrow it would already be old news. I have to find out somehow. I'm looking for contacts," explained Elza with her head under her sweater. In the dark she felt like she wasn't fighting with the sweater, but with her own skin. That by mistake, she'd pulled the skin off her back right over her head. "Sorry it's like this now," she said, thrashing around. Then her boss held her undershirt down with one hand and with the other ripped the turtleneck off her. He saved her life. And the skin on her back would grow back quickly anyway. Of that she was sure. She didn't even have to call anyone.

**Elza.** I've had problems being wedged in since childhood. Whenever I washed my hair in the sink of a cheap hotel, I usually got my head caught between the faucet and the sink basin. The drain was plugged and the water still running and it rose up to my nose and mouth.

On the way to school, in the back of the tram by the window, I leaned against the railing, which followed the wall of the tram car at about a 10-centimeter distance. While I was talking, I stuck my arm in between. When I wanted to get off, I realized that I couldn't pull my arm out. The elbow was too wide. I was wedged in.

"Don't panic. Don't panic, said a group of Polish tourists who were riding with me. The driver closed the door in people's faces and laughed. The Polish people prayed quietly. With every movement, my elbow grew bigger.

The moment they sent Elza to write about the opening of the 3D cinema, she thought of Ian. A few years earlier, he would have been the first to go there, so that his eyes would be opened. A 3D cinema has a three-dimensional screen. The trick is based on shifting the vision of one eye in relation to the other. Since 1999, Ian has only seen out of his right eye. But Elza knew that even if he couldn't be amongst the first viewers, he would surely catch the news in time that this cinema—useless for him—was opening. Because since childhood, Ian had been buying reams of newspapers and magazines. He looked forward to them with unbridled excitement and flipped through them endlessly. Columns and towers of them piled up in his room. He couldn't part with them. In every old magazine it seemed to him there was something extremely interesting that warranted keeping, and he didn't want to give or throw it away. "It's all information," he said to Elza. "I might need them one day."

And Elza admits that Ian truly did always know a ton of interesting facts. While she roasted a chicken, he talked to her about the newest theory of the origin of the universe, about the problems cloned sheep suffer from, about the main character's fate in the documentary film *Nanook* or about a quite new Irish band that had suddenly sold more albums at home than U2.

And while she's taking the chicken out of the oven, Ian says: "And they're opening a 3D cinema here tomorrow. But they definitely won't show any high-quality films. Just some circus attractions, don't you think?" Ian asked and answered himself.

**Elza.** Ian is mine. Ours. We kiss as if it were the first time. Like the first couple who ever kissed. We're a being with one body, two tongues, and three eyes.

At the 3D cinema they were showing a film about dinosaurs. After it finished, Elza never went back to work. Observers considered it to be a stylish end to a career.

In two days she was surprised by a café full of colleagues.

They came to Café Hyena to say good-bye.

"Shoot," Elza wanted to say, shocked.

"Shit," she said instead, unconsciously.

# III
# KALISTO TANZI

**Elza.** Together we ate grapes and washed them down with rosé. The next day I discovered a moist grape stem in my pocket. It looked like an undecorated Christmas tree.

Kalisto Tanzi vanished from the city, which had been hit by a heat wave. The heat radiated from the houses and streets, burning people's faces, and the scorching town seared its brand onto their foreheads.

I stopped in front of the theatre window so I could read Kalisto's name on the posters and confirm to myself that he actually did exist. I enjoy pronouncing his name, which tormented him throughout childhood and puberty and only stopped annoying him after my arrival. I walk slowly to the other end of the city, the muscles in my legs shake slightly in the hot air. It's noon. The only things on the planet that are really moving are drops of sweat. They run down to the base of the nose and then spurt out again under my hair.

I'm going to buy poison.

Ian saw a rat in the crapper last night.

The rat-catcher has a wine cellar underneath his store.

Underground we escape the unbearable heat and drink. He's telling me how intelligent the rats are.

"They have a taster, who tastes food first. When it dies, the others won't even touch the bait. So we now offer the next generation of rat bait. The rat only begins to die four days after consuming the poison. It dies from internal bleeding. Even Seneca confirmed that this sort of death is painless. The other rats think their compatriot has died a natural death. But even so, if several of them die in a short time, they'll evaluate the place as unacceptable because of the high mortality rate and move elsewhere. This gift of judgment is completely missing in some people, or even whole nations."

A perfect, disgusting world. I smile over a glass of Gewurztraminer. The rat-catcher talks very quickly. His face is in constant motion. As if he has too many muscles in it. As if he has a herd of rodents running under his skin. From one ear to the other. From chin to forehead and back. I can feel his restless legs moving under the table and his whole torso sways in a dance.

Looking at him makes me dizzy. My head is spinning as if I were watching a film that cuts too fast from one scene to another. The rat-catcher leans toward me and gets tangled in my hair.

"You're such a pretty little mouse…" he says smiling. I smile too. I feel like I stink of loneliness.

He sees me out. On the way I get a plastic bag full of rat poison. Instead of flowers. I clutch it proudly. Maybe this is how it'll always be, I think. If men want to court me, instead of flowers they'll give me a bag full of second-generation rat bait.

After emerging from the cool cellar, the hot air and a world without Kalisto Tanzi hits me in the face.

The first time I saw Kalisto was at a gallery opening. There was a lot of drinking and during the evening a few new couples emerged. As Ian says—where there are men, women, and alcohol... indicating the coordinates for the location of sex.

I looked into his blue eyes and for the first time I longed for a person with colored eyes. Ian's are almost black. Colors were always a decisive factor for me. Their combination in Kalisto's face attracted me. We sat together and talked till morning. As it always is in the beginning, you can tell your life story again and everything sounds interesting. You talk, slowly revolving around yourself—the whole room dances with you—fine sparkling powder settles in your hair.

In front of Kalisto Tanzi, my talking grew lively. My own life swam in front of our eyes like a glass mountain. With each word, I created it again. Recreated. I was recreated by Kalisto Tanzi. You could write a book about it, indeed! It would be a musical: *Oh little fairy—if you only knew what I've been through...*

But it's already lunchtime. I'm sitting in the café. Wearing a brown dress: an old lady. I'm sitting opposite Ian. An old couple. The silence between us is interrupted only by new headlines. Ian reads them to me from time to time over the table. And then reads on. Sometimes he folds the paper and looks into my face. Our eyes don't meet. The wine tastes like prunes and chocolate. The Coca-Cola logo on the tablecloth stealthily begins to rise toward my face. I weigh it down with a plate. I like when everything stays in its place.

At home I sit at the table and write a letter to Kalisto. Ian is standing at my back—Jeez, do you have to write such a long letter, you poor thing? Wouldn't a text be enough? For example: Where are you?

Kalisto Tanzi has no mobile or email address. He considers that kind of communication threatening.

There's no simple way to intervene in his life, climb through the window on the screen or display, materialize right in front of his eyes. Elza couldn't rely on electronic seduction. Although she had a talent for it—for chatting and sweet nothings. She was a clever rhapsodist.

But the new possibilities brought her strong competition. It was so easy to get entangled with someone, to get in contact. Everything played in favor of seduction. Especially the time saved by rapid communication.

No one had to patrol a dark street at night, travel in a coach, a car, a storm. Repair wheels, change the boiling water in the radiator, march around the neighborhoods and cafés, circle helplessly in the city streets where there might be a hope of meeting the beloved one. Map the possibility of their being there. Follow, stalk, hide, stay motionless for years or journey constantly.

Emails and quick texts were windows and mirrors rapidly multiplying in the world. You could crawl through into a room, onto the roof, the bathroom, underwater, take flight. Hang your own alluring picture anywhere—an installation.


**Elza.** Into the air, in your way. Expose you to my picture.


Elza's morning begins with writing. She puts on some music and works on her book intensely for half an hour. While she's writing, she often stands up from the chair, sweating, because as she writes, she drinks liters of tea, turns the music up too loud, and writes and writes. She writes as if she were running downhill. She sweats and it chills her. Her whole life, her body temperature has varied between 37.1 and 37.6 degrees Celsius and this translates to a slight tremor and weak nerves. In addition to making you creative and passionate in bed, a fever allows you to stay home undisturbed. Doctors are usually afraid to send a patient with a fever into the whirlwind of a workday.

When she finishes writing, she's hungry, thirsty, and has no more attention span. Elza lacks the ability to focus on creative work for a longer time—*sitzfleisch*. Her workday lasts three hours. When Elza rises from the desk, Ian gets out of bed. They sit together on the sofa in the kitchen and think about what to eat and what Elza will go buy. They usually eat sandwiches and drink gin and grapefruit juice. Elza read that 80% of how a person feels comes from their stomach. From what's in it. Sandwiches and gin are food you'd associate with celebrations. That's why whole years of her life seemed to her like one big continuous celebration. Day after day. And, as it happens during any genuinely enjoyed, seriously done celebration—at dusk or dawn, when the light is uncertain for a long time and the countryside reminds you of a theatrically lit stage set, somewhere at the root of the tongue and on the palate, a decent bitter taste appears—the taste of the end of a celebration. It's room temperature, full-bodied, with a fruity bouquet and a long tail. At night it woke her up more and more often: the taste of a sad ending. Like on New Year's Eve when a few seconds before midnight Ian goes outside with another woman and on Elza's chest, head, and shoulders squats a hairy troll: a nightmare, and he pisses, hot, right onto her flat breasts.


On the way home at dawn, Elza burst into tears in the middle of the street.

"I don't want to march. I don't want to keep marching on! All my life I've done nothing but march on!"

"Then we don't have to walk. I'll call a taxi," says Ian, soothing her.

"You don't understand. It doesn't matter. On foot or by taxi. All we do is just keep marching on!"


**Elza.** But actually it was the marching that kept me awake. Some dealt with problems in our city by walking, others by swimming, galloping on a horse, or shooting.

"Where are you going, Elza? Aha. Just walking around, are you? Me too. But where? You don't want to tell me, do you? I had a friend, he never wanted to tell me either. He just leaned over to me and whispered: You know, friend, I'm just on my way to *the place*. So you just say the same, Elza. That you are going to *the place*."

It's a small city. The minute you start off, you've already got most of it behind you. Someone who wants to stroll has to go round in circles—like a carousel horse—and on his way he bumps into other merry-go-rounds.

We stroll to avoid company and patiently, step by step, to evoke a feeling of freedom. In reality, we're members of a carousel sect with rigid rules of the circle.


I prefer to jump into the pool. Arms and legs working like two mill wheels. My breathing gets faster, deeper, and constant. Smaller and larger pools in my head gradually fill with swimmers: alternately racing and drowning, diving and floating.

Today there are too many people at the pool. I barely avoid first the arms opening wide under the water and then the kicking legs. In the middle, children stand in a circle throwing a ball full of sand back and forth. From the pool wall the fat legs of a woman exercising shoot out toward me. In the locker room a blind girl uncertainly changes into her swimsuit. My teeth go numb. As if I've been hit in the face with the stick.

Opposite the exit from the pool is Kalisto Tanzi's apartment. It never leaves my gaze. This summer I'm not leaving the city. Not seeking a change of scene. Not looking for the sea. I cling to the windows of an abandoned apartment.

Ian and I meet by chance in the city. We drink wine the entire long summer evening. He tells me how he used to think that he'd somehow remember his whole life in more detail. "Whole parts, whole slabs, have disappeared. And events don't move into the distance in a linear way with the passing time. It's not a straight line, it's a serpentine one. Some sections, miles from each other in time, come together at the bends, the curves intersect and suddenly a glimmer rises up above the surface: an arm bent at the elbow, wet hair, a fogged-up window, a mouth shaped like a circle tense on the inhale." I tell Ian what I read today about a dangerous disease. It breaks out in middle age and the main sign is that the person begins to dance. "Then all you need is to find some good music to go with it," says Ian.


Ian brought Elza to the taxi stand in an effort to avoid another bottle of wine and a march through the hot nighttime city. He sat her down next to the driver and looked into the man's face. He himself stayed standing on the sidewalk. He closed Elza's door and his arms remained hanging helplessly at his sides, useless and too long. He had to take care not to drag them on the ground. Not to step on them.


In a moment, the taxi stops at the end of the street and lets Elza out. She jumps out like a deer. Submerges herself back into the city. Opens her arms, kicks her legs. The man on the sidewalk looks at her back as she moves into the distance and starts to dance. The orchestra's not playing.

Kalisto Tanzi, Elza sings. That's the name of the small, cuddly animal that's lazily growing in me. Sings Elza. And women would like to buy it for their men and men set their eye on it. They look at me and see it, sitting inside, ripening. Sings Elza. Right on the other side of the door. And they'd like to split open my belly and break my back in two. Just so they can reach it. Sings Elza. They'd like to tear off my head and fish inside with their hands. Sings Elza. Not minding the blood: happily, even in front of the children. Elza sings.


Kalisto Tanzi's apartment remains empty even after his return. He spends most of his time in the car. As a dancer at the peak of his career, he barely moves when off stage. Driving a car helps him overcome inertia. The scenery goes by at a speed comparable to when you're dancing. The car forms the bottom half of Kalisto's body. His back grows out of the driver's seat. Kalisto Tanzi is a minotaur. When I approach him, I slip into the car's interior as if into a tight embrace.

When Kalisto and Elza hug, she thinks of the warm, rubbery internal organs handed around by kids in classrooms when they learned about the human body. She and Kalisto are the pulsing innards of the dark vehicle. The car's liver. Paired organs. Kidneys. They work all night. Warmly dressed in a car that's cooling down. Their movements keep the vehicle alive.


In the morning she came back through empty streets. Washed white by a tidal wave: first it took all the houses and city with it. Then it grabbed people by the legs. And in two days it returned them: faces scrubbed by hard sand, a pearl in every orifice.

At home she lay down beside Ian's sleeping face. It revealed the whole chain of appearances he had passed through in his life. Friends from childhood, an endlessly long summer, parents, a bicycle wheel peeking out from under the Christmas tree. Changes for the better as well as decay. Ian's face was ageless. It was a restless swarm that had alighted in one place.

When she looked into his eyes, she saw all their common permutations. Every couple they'd ever been.


Her pain woke her up. It shot from elbow to palm and in the opposite direction to her shoulder. It agitated Elza. It was caused by her unnatural position in the car.

Kalisto ruled her life. When she walked down the city streets, she no longer looked at the faces of pedestrians, but into the cars. She was looking for Kalisto Tanzi's driving body. Instead of the sidewalk she would have preferred to walk in the middle of the road along the yellow line between the cars.

At times her arm became quite weak. She couldn't work with it. (*Don't panic*, Elza probably thought, *don't panic*.)

She couldn't hold anything in her hand. Her fingers went numb. Her arm dried out and hung by her side like the sign of an eternal presence—Kalisto Tanzi was always at her side; when she couldn't write with it, when a pot slipped from her fingers. If she needed the arm, but couldn't use it, she shivered with pleasure.

She stopped eating sandwiches—only grapefruit juice and gin, apple and calvados, whisky on the rocks, remained. It seemed to her distasteful to eat. To have chewed food in her mouth. She wanted her mouth to be empty and noble—prepared to receive. His mouth.

She disinfected herself with gin and at the same time it gave her the courage and insolence to meet with someone whom she liked so much. To look into the face that threatened her with what she longed for. The gin made it more bearable and livable. It was also the answer for what to do with her free time. With the inertia of the night just before dawn.

When Elza was desperate, she regretted never having learned to do a cartwheel. For example, she could pass the time that way while she was waiting for Kalisto Tanzi. If she could do them around the perimeter of the parking lot, her day would definitely pass faster. As it was, she just went round and round in ordinary loops.

But then she saw his car. It was sitting at the very back of the lot—that's why she didn't notice. She opened the door and crawled onto the seat. She turned her face, however, toward a strange man. "Honey, this isn't the time. You can see I have my daughter in the back." Elza turned her head toward the back and looked at the little girl sitting there. "Maybe next time," the man said, kicking her out of the car.

She had to tell someone.

That evening she described the event to Ian as a story that had happened to her *Friend*. She had saved this character of *Friend*. It would definitely come in handy sometime. Later, she read that lonely children who have no siblings often have imaginary friends.

This way, over time, Elza told Ian about the *Friend*, who began to behave much like Kalisto Tanzi. They had common opinions, friends, and pasts. They went to the same schools and restaurants. They read the same books.

Over time, Elza told Ian almost everything about Kalisto Tanzi this way.

Rebeka had an imaginary friend only during childhood. She disappeared after her first menstruation. Her name was Yp. And besides her, Rebeka took care of imaginary animals as well—one very small and fast dog, two ladybugs, and a golden horse who was completely white.

Wolfgang Elfman, brother of Lukas Elfman, had his animals in the forest. They were wild. So he couldn't raise them in the apartment. He always went to them in the forest. He called to them and they came running. Then they played together and talked until it got dark.

When Lukas was a little boy, he wanted to play with them too. But Wolfgang never invited him to visit the animals. He always just told him in the evening about all the things they had done together during the day. He was excited and his eyes shone in the dark room. Lukas Elfman decided that he would find the animals himself.

"Woooolfgaaaang's animals!" he called out in the middle of the wood. "Woooolfgaaaang's animals!" he yelled and went deeper and deeper in.

Elza plunged into the forest. After a while she stopped and turned her face toward the crowns of the trees. "Kaaaliiistooo Taaanziii," she called. "Kaaaliiistooo Taaanziii," she shouted and headed deeper and deeper into the wood. The crowns of the trees shone on the surface. The water swallowed movement and words. With an open mouth she hit the bottom of the lake.

**(The End)**

# IV
# SUMMER

During the summer, Elza and Rebeka kept missing each other. They only met once a month at the Hyena when Rebeka paid Elfman, Elza, and Ian their stipends. The Trinity had already given up their regular meetings. It was time for them to create on their own. Elza didn't read aloud from *Seeing People Off* anymore. Ian read from it to himself, quietly. "Just wait till I write a book about love," threatened Elza.

Rebeka earned money as a tennis line judge. She sat on the court and fixed her eyes on the white line in the clay. It reminded her of the times she'd been mushroom picking with her father. The difference was that when looking for mushrooms, your eyes rove around for the trophy, while a line judge just keeps them trained on one place. It's the trophy that's moving. Rebeka had the same relationship with mushrooms that a woman has with flowers. Their smell and color impressed her. Plus, mushrooms had a body. Volume. They could be picked up, squeezed.

**Rebeka.** Mushrooms could be eaten. The only member of the family who didn't like them was Grandma. When she was little, the family next door was poisoned eating a mushroom omelet. Grandma always told this story of the poisoned family when we were eating mushrooms. She sat at the head of the table over an empty plate and smoothed the tablecloth with her hands.

"The pain was so bad the children scratched the plaster right off the walls..."

"Well, I can't get enough of these mushrooms today," said father, taking them in regular intervals from the pan.

"They took them to the hospital, but it was too late, no one could help them. They all died. Two adults and three children. From the mushrooms."

Grandma was also a seeker. A spiritual hitchhiker. She sniffed around for tennis balls.

In the morning we used to go shopping at a store that was right next to the courts. Grandma taught me to comb through the grass on the path. Sometimes a ball hit by a clumsy tennis player would go over the fence and drop here. Then it was ours. Grandma noticed that in many places the fence surrounding the courts had been pulled up. Just enough for a child's hand to reach under it. You could get a lot of used balls under there. We could pick and choose. Yellow or white. Grandma chose only clean furry ones. The gray scuffed ones that tennis players call spuds we left untouched.

The art of being a line judge is that for hours you don't take your eyes off of one spot and never start thinking about anything else. In the judge's mind, no image comes up, he doesn't dream, think, remember, or deduce. In his head icons don't light up. His mind creates no desktop background: autumn woods, the universe, the stars, planets, a child's face. The screensaver doesn't come on.

The line judge doesn't waver, he keeps his gaze balanced on the thin white rope. Glued to the boundary. His gaze burns at every point on the straight line. The line judge lives on the equator—he sweats and freezes. He doesn't imagine scenes of countries, cities, the sea, or rain. In his mind he doesn't talk to anyone, kiss, argue, or polemicize.

His empty brain waits only for balls. He lies in wait like a well-combed lawn, like children with their grandparents on the other side of the court fence.


When Rebeka returned from work, she sat down at the window and waited for the snippets of Elfman walking. For his body, passing behind the drawn blinds—frame by frame like a feature-length film.

"I have such an unpleasant feeling, as if she were always eyeing me," complained Elfman to Elza in July.


**Elfman.** Yesterday, for example, we were lying in bed, watching television. Suddenly Rebeka leaned over me, looking silently into my face. "What are you doing?" I asked her.

"I'm looking to see if you're sleeping."

"I'm not sleeping, I'm watching."

"So then why are your eyes closed?"

"They're not closed—you can't watch me all the time."

"I'm not watching you, I'm noticing you."

At three in the morning she woke me up with a smack. She was still watching television. Some film had just ended. Rebeka was watching the closing credits, fascinated. They seemed endless. She grabbed my face in her hands and shouted: "Look!

Look! Look how many people made money off of one film! And one more, more, more!" Rebeka shouted.

"Go to sleep, you watch too much television."

"I can't sleep," Rebeka smiled. "I'm haunted by that eternal inertia. It's three o' clock and morning isn't coming. The only things moving on this planet are those credits."

(In reality, Elfman used at least two obscenities in every instance of direct speech. Usually right at the beginning of the sentence.)

At three in the morning Elza got out of the car. Now every day was New Year's Eve. She and Kalisto Tanzi sat in the parked car and drank red wine. Elza had her arms around his neck and looked searchingly into his face. She couldn't get enough of looking at it.

When she got home, it was already dark in the apartment. It was dawn and cool outside. She cut herself a slice of bread and peeled a clove of garlic. She leaned against the radiator and munched. The taste of garlic overwhelmed everything. The smell of Kalisto Tanzi's mouth, Elza's unfulfilled desire. Slowly she warmed herself. She smiled like one would in the evening after a day of skiing.

At three in the morning her pleasure peaked. The pleasure of unfulfillment and non-culmination. Of the continual, uneasy eruption. Of the endless tension of an unsatiated being.

Elza marched all night—with the same sharp steps. Without a break. She loved the minotaur. They progressed together through the labyrinth.

(Desire that is satiable isn't true desire, they sing in one Armenian chanson.) When she looked into Kalisto's eyes, she saw a smaller version of her own face. A small portrait of a pin-like head.

Then they parted and she went to lie down next to a sleeping Ian. Now she only saw him with closed eyes. She liked him. In spite of everything. She wound her withering arm around his neck. Like thread through a maze.

Ian slept deeply. The book that devoured his days exhausted him at night with heavy dreams. In them he took care of very small children who continually got lost. And Elza was always leaving him for some important work meetings. And he just sat in the old café or in the desolate bar where his father had taken him once when he was on the brink of adulthood. He just sat there, as if he were weeping.

At home he separated himself from Elza. In the apartment he made himself a smaller apartment of his own. He divided the space with cupboards and armchairs, and made a roof out of a blue sheet. It wasn't the cleanest. On it were the visible crusty whitish remains of lovemaking. They sat above his head like clouds in summer. Dog days.

It reminded Elza of times when she'd been obsessed with building dwellings. During childhood she and her brother built them together. From mattresses and armchairs in the children's bedroom. Or in the garden among three currant bushes covered on top with foil. One lived well in the tops of trees too, pear or walnut. Exceptionally spacious and luxurious was the living space under the creeping vines. The vines cascaded onto the ground rich and thick like African dreadlocks and formed a generous private space between the stem and the branches. A place for meditation, a space for life.

In the little house Ian wrote and watched a small black and white television. The volume control was broken, so you couldn't get an optimal sound level. It either blared or whispered. Ian watched all seventeen channels one by one. He argued with the moderators out loud and shouted over the commentators.

From the other side of the wall Elza heard agitated voices, political commentary, squealing brakes, explosions, and the sound of crumpling metal and windshields shattering onto the sidewalks and floors of cars. She felt like Ian's house was full of people, loud places and shops where people stood in long sweaty lines.

When Rebeka managed to levitate a shot glass at Café Hyena on Wednesday, she thought that her telekinesis abilities would save her life. She wouldn't have to earn money. She hoped that this ability to move things with a focused gaze would secure the entire Quartet financially. They would leave the city and live in a little house by the sea. On one of the Greek islands. Preferably Patmos.

Her telekinesis was, however, too humble and inconspicuous. Everything she trapped in her gaze moved only very slightly, almost imperceptibly. "Three out of five people can do this. They just don't know about it," the experts stated after testing her. A disappointed Rebeka closed her eyes from the pain.

In the darkness under her eyelids glowed silhouettes of her imaginary friends from childhood—Yp and a very small and fast dog. They hadn't seen each other for ages.

At Café Hyena they started playing the tango. Elza and Ian clenched each other so tightly on the dance floor that they had to hold their breath. And they danced more and more wildly, fire in their eyes, sparks flying under their heels. They leaned back from the waist, each in a different direction. Their bodies fused to the midpoint, then blooming like the sepal of a flower.

"Have you ever seen Elza and Ian dance like that?" Rebeka asked Elfman.

"Never," he whispered.

Elza and her man danced, their lips firmly closed and streams of sweat running down their spines. Slow and thick like blood. Like slim, graceful snakes. They danced passionately and wildly. They danced as if they were stamping on something underground. Some lost image, a dead couple, each other. Damn music.


There are two women at the next table. Sitting opposite one another. "But you always wanted to have a big house full of children," says one, while the other has a sad smile on her face. Elza had never heard a different combination.


**Elza.** A dream of a small apartment full of children or being alone in a huge house. I've never heard of such wishes. To be left alone in a huge house. Alone with the echo. In every room, behind every door. So many times alone. Okay, maybe—with a bottle of alcohol at most. Every day new and new again. Renewing every day like the sun, which should be different, new every day. Like the delicate French girl who, in the end, changed into a toad. Into a wise old woman in love with her house. Nothing else was left. Everyone had died. Only the house was immortal. Heavy and hulking, a slightly clumsy lover. Every room in it smelled different. But all of them together reeked of old age. She couldn't fall asleep in it. Until she had gotten completely drunk. And even then, men with skin torn instead of clothes endlessly rustled around in the rooms, bumping into furniture.

Elza was washing the floor. Ian sat on the couch and read aloud. When Elza finished, she stood up and raised her arms like bird's wings. "Done," she wanted to say gaily. "Damn," she said unconsciously.

(No one noticed.)

Rebeka traveled to the center of the city. It was Sunday—the city was empty and desolate. Only sad backdrops remained. She sat in the tram and opposite her was a man with a baby in a carriage. The baby's tongue was hanging out, the pupils in his eyes rolling around quickly in random elliptical patterns. His whole face was a mockery, a parody of babyhood itself. The father looked like the enemy of every living thing.

The city was lit with matte light and only tourists and freaks moved through the empty streets. Monsters—Sunday is their day. They ride around in trams, sit by fountains. They sleep for a while, then shout and curse. The cobblestones are covered with slime that they leave behind like snails. With stickiness, they mark their territory. On Monday morning their tracks are spread around town on the soles of bank tellers', advertising agents', and City Hall bureaucrats' shoes. They carry them into glass office buildings, wipe them on shag carpets, and on the fur of a polar bear rug under the coffee table. And the city is clean again—bright and shiny like the paw of a prehistoric animal licked clean.

And the rockers can once again play their stuff: walk baby, talk baby… And the misfits slip away—fading back behind the walls of working people, growing in the streets like wild meat.


In front of the Hyena, Rebeka ran into young Ginsberg. He was smoking, singing, and dancing a little. "Out for a stroll? Hm. But give it to me straight, they're paying you, right? Really, nothing? Free? I get paid. A thousand for a Sunday round of the city, five hundred during workdays. I make money that way on weekends. I work the city. Create an image. An attractive look, things going on, life in the streets, the pulse of the city. It's very important to the mayor for people to be in the streets, strolling around, for the city to look alive. As if the inhabitants couldn't live without the city, couldn't bear to sit at home. Slovaks are a modern nation, something's always drawing them out into the streets and to local pubs. City Hall is trying hard. It's like a policy. Because of the tourists. So they won't feel lonely. So they won't be afraid."


"We got screwed pretty good. We just walk around and everyone else is getting paid for it," said Rebeka to Elza.

"Oh come on, we stroll around because we like to."

"I don't feel good anymore knowing that I do it for free and others are getting paid. We got screwed."

"Don't be silly," Elza laughed.

To Rebeka her laughter seemed suspicious. Paid for. Is she in on it with them? She asked herself that question over and over with every person she saw out at night in the city. She began to notice people in the cafés. The guests at Café Hyena too. They look so tired. They sit there bored like at work. And it's the same ones. You could lose your mind: always the same faces. Sometimes they mix it up. Pairs switch partners, families switch children or grandparents. At the beginning of the week someone is a loner lost in thought and by Thursday he's already sitting at a packed table without enough chairs to go around. They're paying them too, wailed Rebeka. The people in the cafés and bars. They're playing us. They're creating the city. Filling the space, taking seats.


"A while ago, a man stopped by my house first thing in the morning," said Rebeka to Elza. "He introduced himself as Sabato and brought me a bag full of colored balls, including soccer balls, volleyballs, a few tennis balls, and a swarm of golf and ping-pong balls, which had flown over the fence into his yard during my childhood. There was also a billiard ball and two small roulette balls. When he'd collected them, first he went to the famous Argentinian writer, J.L. Borges, because he thought it was *he* who'd been throwing them into the yard on purpose the whole time. Sabato, in fact, always held Borges responsible for all the bad that happened to him in life. I identified all the balls found as mine. I thanked him and apologized for having had such bad aim so often in childhood. The whole time Sabato didn't lift his gaze from that heap of round objects. Then he turned on his heel and blurted: "My God Miss, so many shots in the dark!""

"You've already told me that story," said Elza. "Yesterday morning on the phone."

"I don't remember that, but you're probably right. I think it'll be another one of my obsessive stories. Since I started earning, I've already collected twelve of them. Twelve stories that make me tell them over and over again. With most of them, my friends already start interrupting me halfway through. They signal that they already know them. They look away, greet some stranger with a nod of the head, another one with an ardent hug, or start rummaging around for a biscuit in a deep, dark bag. But their search is fruitless because they gobbled it up long ago. And that story is left lying there, that is, only the half that's been told already, on the ground, like some dirty crumpled piece of underwear full of biological material, or one laceless shoe in a meter-high snowdrift on the way to the pub. There's no sadder sight, believe me."


Rebeka sat with Elza and the guys at Hyena, but she felt like she was spending money with strangers. Out of politeness, in the evening, she drank pear schnapps so she'd be good company.

Gregarious, lively. In the morning she exercised, ate yogurt, and then cried for a long time in the shower. Her skin turned completely red from the hot water.

In the evening, she sat with her friends. The face of the woman sitting opposite seemed to her unbearably close. She smiled, but was afraid she couldn't control the corners of her mouth. She was afraid of twitching. Rebeka realized she'd already been sitting in front of the mirror for years. During that time the contours of her face had sagged toward the ground. The skin on her chin and flesh on her jaw had grown slack. Gravity was pulling her features toward the floor. She paid the bill for the Quartet, and when she went out into the cool air, it surprised her how quickly a girl can turn into an institution.

At the end of the street a glimpse of a familiar back. Rebeka picked up the pace: Yp was out for a walk. At her side was a very small and fast dog.


She walked quickly along the quay. The city breathed calmly and deeply. Only once in a while she could hear a distant: PING...

PING... PINGPING... PINGPINGPING... PING from the supermarket. People were shopping. The codes at the checkout were jumping onto the receipts with a crackling sound. Like a fire. The cashiers were doing their thing. I imagined the Earth turning in the universe, almost silently. Except for that continual signal, a symphony of PING... PING... PINGPING... PINGPINGPING... PING.


Elza and Ian were swimming at the lake. Elza was torn from her regular stroke by a scream. She turned onto her back so she could see the shore. A boy from the village was standing there with a scooter. Bashing it against the ground. His face red with anger. "Fucking hell, you can't ride on these forest paths. I'm gonna fuckin' lay down some goddamn concrete blocks here. I swear to God, I'll fuckin' lay some down," he yelled.

When they got out of the lake, Ian looked at his naked wet belly. Water was streaming down it.

"Tears are running down my belly," he pointed out to Elza.

On the beach more and more blankets started to crowd them in. Luckily, it was only from the sides and not from above. They preferred not to wait until they were dry. Her man pulled his pants on over a wet bathing suit. They were soaked through after he'd walked around for a little while. This moistness created lots of small localized maps, which became one big map over time. In the bus no one crowded them. On the contrary, the whole front part was empty. It was just them and the driver. Elza sat and her man stood.

"I'm drying myself," he said, leaning his map against her shoulder. Approximately where Canada might be.

When the bus went over the bridge, from the window they saw the river. Rising. For a moment she felt it in her shoes. She wiggled her toes. The water smacked its lips with every step.

Like big animals watching a herd of smaller ones. Like a big animal a moment before eating.

Many singers sing about how nostalgia settles over them at night. With Ian it was hunger. First he would walk resolutely and then more and more slowly around the kitchen. The change in rhythm signals loneliness. As Elza's stride becomes more and more abrupt and quick, he slows down. It reminds her of childhood and walks with Mama, who limped. When she read French fairytales, they had characters called Princess Limpetta and Prince Limper. Mama told her: That's about me, I'm Limpetta.

Now she had found Limper too. Tensely, she imagined the moment when the rhythm of their pulse, the thumping of their blood, would change too. When they would slowly grow farther from each other with their banging and beating. Their duet changing to voice and echo and then definitively to first and second voice: nostalgiaaaaaa.

"These cookies are half as thick as they used to be," called Ian from the kitchen. And that unfortunate sentence, like a quick shot, irretrievably launched their old age together.

She asked him to sit down by her—on the bed. She put her arms around his neck and kissed him. He opened his lips only after a moment. He wound his arm around her knee and with one smooth movement—in one breath—he moved her from the bed to his arms. She sat there completely still. As if up in the crown of a tree. In a place from where you could see everything, while staying unseen. She held on now with her whole body.

Ian's long arms reminded Elza of a creeping vine. He often stroked them absent-mindedly while telling her a story. Long and tangled.

Kalisto brought Elza a stone from the bottom of the ocean. She put it on the table at home. (A stone from the *Friend*). A beautiful stone. Kalisto said it was a perfect human face: eyes, mouth, nose. Ian put it by the telephone and stuck two pencils into each of its eyes.

On the way back from the lake, Ian and Elza sat down in a village pub. While they drank, the place filled up. At five, a local band began to play—the daughter played the synthesizer and the father sang. On the wooden fence behind the stage, hanging musical lights blinked. They reflected off old bicycle frames parked by the wall.

On the dance floor a couple of children were busy colliding with each other. *I am a New York City Boy*—carried up over the village pub's yard.

Elza and her man were joined by film director Wang and his student Sang-Fun. "I come to these village events for work," said Wang, smiling. "I'm looking for usable human characters here." Ian had met him by chance some time earlier at a Prague antique shop. Wang was sitting over a box of old photographs. "I'm looking for my characters," he had said then with his head in the box.

"I want to shoot a film about what pisses your generation off,"
said Sang-Fun the student, asking Ian to dance.
"Nothing pisses me off anymore," said Ian.

The cookies in the retail network shrank further, irretrievably.

PING... PING... PINGPING... PINGPINGPING...
PING... . PING... PING... PINGPING...
PINGPINGPING... PING.

Elza saw Sang-Fun again. They met by chance after the pre-
miere of a ballet where Kalisto Tanzi danced the main role.
Sang-Fun took Elza downtown in her car. At that time, she
didn't want to make films anymore. She was the spokeswoman
for Shakespeare, a company that made fishing supplies. "This is
how I make my living, but otherwise—I write. Although right
now I only have a few picturesque episodes. Last Christmas I
finished a novel. I didn't want to publish it here. Publishing work
in Slovakia doesn't make sense. I approached an English publisher. They wrote to me, saying I should send a 30-page excerpt
in English. So I sent it and waited. And what do you think happened next? In six months *The Da Vinci Code* came out. Based
on my excerpt," laughed Sang-Fun bitterly. "But you see, time
heals everything. The book lives a life of its own. And now I'm
not even pissed off anymore. Between Wang and me it stopped
working too. But he still makes films. They're the kind of films
where police chase murderers and murderers chase victims. But
it always takes so long that after a while you realize you truly
don't give a damn whether they catch them and kill them. They

run and scream, but you don't root for them. Not for the murderers or the victims or the police. You don't care. You just want it to end already."

The only exception was the film *Submarine T437*, which Wang shot based on a true story. It joined the ranks of those disaster films that take place inside the numbing environment of a submarine. Something's always dripping in there and on the valves there are drops of water forming dramatically.

# V
# AUTUMN

A strange boy joined Elza on her way home. By chance. Their strides coming into sync. It was the last day of August and the next day he'd have to go back to school again. When he smiled at her, she offered him a cigarette. She shouldn't have. She saw this when he tore a Coca-Cola can into strips with his bare hands. The boy explained that he wanted to study low-voltage but his asshole parents were making him study high-voltage at school. Finally, Elza overcame her cowardice and said good-bye. The stranger still managed to bite her on the neck.

Ian was already in his pajamas. She poured herself a whisky as disinfectant. She called Rebeka. Listened to her voice as it ran through her body. It warmed her.

In bed Ian read Elza a story about jackals. In the story they claimed to be powerless. That they could express good and evil only through their teeth. "That's odd," said Elza. "Recently a strange boy bit my *Friend* in the neck on the street."

"When you left, I sat in the car. I couldn't go home. Then I drove there—the long way, down your street," said Kalisto, hugging Elza tightly around her wounded neck.

"Every day, everything I do—is just a dance to meet you halfway," said Elza, smiling with her teeth pressed against Kalisto's mouth. Behind his back a brown current of water was reflected in her eyes. It was autumn. The Danube was rising.

In the evening, Rebeka and Elza sat alone in the café. They slowly sipped from a common glass of wine. Rebeka was already clearly drunk.

"God Rebeka, you get drunk from one glass of wine," moaned Elza.

"Don't be stupid. You're making me into an alcoholic who gets drunk from one glass. Actually, I have a whole bottle of calvados in my purse. Don't worry, I start drinking first thing in the morning. I drink and stroll along the quay."

Ian sat at the table, eating dinner. His dumplings first slipped into the water and then turned to stone. When Elza lied, Ian's face froze. She remembered a card, which Jehovah's Witnesses carry with them in case of an accident. Instructions to the doctor: no blood!

The Danube was rising again. People stopped going to work—they just walked along the river instead. It was coming up closer and closer to their faces. They stopped noticing the buildings and mirrors—some left their families so that they could walk all day along the river, getting closer and closer to them day after day. It was coming up to meet them. Its humid, pulsing breath beat in their heads at night. It stung. They sucked it deep into their lungs. Swayed lightly while they watched its ferocious current.

Elza sits alone in the café. Rebeka didn't come. Something came up. (Probably Yp and the very small and fast dog.) "What should I do if I love two men?" a young woman asked her girlfriend helplessly at the next table. "Write a novel," said Elza turning toward her. "Make it a story where there's little talk and a lot of sorrow."

The river draws closer and closer to the stream of gawking people. They jump onto the sandbags so they can see themselves in it. And at night they dream dreams on the shore. Dreams in which clouds of dust whirl behind herds of galloping animals.

"My knees hurt so much that I can't even hold the slimmest woman on my lap. Or a child. Nothing. I can't even put a thicker book on my knees. Only a newspaper. And my joints! And soul! And that weirdness! I see it in myself—I'm weirder and weirder every day. I used to be happy and all. But now I'm just sort of weird. Constantly. Today, though, I felt like working again. That morning air, morning sun, and morning cognac were really good for me. Today I'll be going around in circles until evening," said Kalisto Tanzi, laughing.

In twelve hours, he would hug Elza with his arm around her shoulders. After midnight he always drives with only one hand. Elza explains the feeling of whoooosh.

"When I drive down Heyduk Street and *someone runs out of the dental surgery with a handkerchief pressed to their cheek instead of a phone*, I feel sorry for them and hug them in my mind. In reality, though, I actually just miss them, I lean back until there's that quiet swoosh and I think to myself—whooooosh, I've avoided it so far. All that pain and suffering. Whooooosh, and I breathe a sigh of relief that I'm not in their shoes."

"I do it in waiting areas. I thread my way through people, avoiding them only by a hair. I swish by, stirring up the air and sighing with every stem christie: whoooosh... I dodge, even if the contours are clear in the distance. I feel like I'm dancing, twirling toward them."

Rebeka's gaze couldn't be avoided. "I saw it in you. The change. Your face is different and you've stopped eating. You can barely move your arm. As if it were wedged somewhere independently of your body," said Rebeka to Elza on the phone.

"You sniff out everything," Elza jumped in, panicking.

"I just feel sorry for Ian and actually for you. Actually for everyone. I pity all of you. You should get a job instead."

Whoooosh—thought Elza to herself. In the dark, Kalisto Tanzi's car barely missed Ian's body.

Ian was walking toward the quay. He recognized Rebeka's back from a distance. She was standing right at the flood wall.

Intensely watching the surface of the river. It seemed like an endless straight line. Rebeka inhaled deeply, as if together with the humid night air she wanted to take in the time zone of the quay as well. Time here passed differently than on the tennis court, differently than for people in cars, and had a completely different tempo than at the hospital above the river. There the hands of the clock move like a magnetized needle in a compass. Motionless for years, it turns constantly. Rebeka and Ian nodded to each other, and Ian walked on. He moved slowly. As if he were carrying in his body a unique, but very fragile constellation, which he didn't want to disturb. So that the images didn't mix with one another. He breathed shallowly, avoiding exertion, walking up hills, or sudden movements. As if he had a lottery bin in his belly. Numbered balls, that weren't allowed to move from their places, or touch each other, Rebeka thought to herself about Ian's innards.

Kalisto Tanzi knelt at Elza's feet and kissed her pants. She looked at the crown of the head of a man who liked fabric. He loved fully-dressed women. They sat for months in the car. Submerging their faces in each other's sweaters and hair. Kalisto basically never wanted to go to an apartment, to bed.

For the first time, we took off all our clothes. Kalisto Tanzi said: "I feel so relaxed! Now I've got everything in the world."

She knew they were in trouble. It was a lovely view, watching him lie down naked on his back. He put his legs in the exact position a baby does when you change its diaper. A defenseless position. Despite this, she diligently searched the white body of the minotaur. But found nothing she desired.

She stroked his back. Slowly and tenderly. More with wonder than love. With wonder at how she had loved this body so much that she'd held on for hours in the snow in the parking lot waiting for it. How for this she had lost her mind for a whole winter and summer and had pressed her face into the dirt in the garden.

In the car Kalisto Tanzi regained his balance. He left the motor running even in the parking lot, ran the heater and wondered out loud why the quality of Tom and Jerry's performances had gone down over the last few years and whether they were now performing without joy, just for money.

**Elza.** The windshield shattered and the glass flew into our faces. And one of the smaller windows exploded too. Then Ian stepped back from the car and *song&dance* gradually moved away.

It was precisely this, which evoked the biggest confusion and terror in me—stellar, endless, universal terror. The idea that it would end with Kalisto Tanzi and I holding hands in the car and talking and suddenly, all at once, the only thing left of him would be a leg and a hand and I would see into his belly. And then I didn't know what would be more terrifying—that he no longer existed or the thing he had turned into. All those tangled tubes, utility networks—soft and flexible like slimy vacuum hoses, pipes in the ugliest parts of houses, in the neglected basements of hospitals—the ones that made me stop smoking. On them you could smell those cigarettes that pregnant women and dying old men had gone there to smoke secretly. They smelled helpless, like blood—metallic.

Like that heavy gray table I'm sitting at a week later with Kalisto Tanzi, drinking fragrant Metaxa. One after the other like Alice drinking her potion, but it's completely useless, because I don't feel like sticking my hands under Kalisto's shirt or in his pants, and he feels it, and a helpless smile is spreading to the corners of his face. Wider and wider.

And he's ordering cognac and one bowl of soup after another and the table between us is shaking like his legs down under the deck, like Kalisto's helpless tied-up-in-knots stomach. And I see myself a couple of months before starting to shake when I saw his shirt hanging over my chair. And my body didn't exist when he wasn't looking at it.


The river was back in its bed again. On the banks, mud-combed grass was drying. The stone with the poked out eyes that had just hurtled through the window fell back onto the bottom of Kalisto's car. That's probably all that remained after the flood.


Yp sat on the wall. Stroking a very small and fast dog.


**(The Second End)**

# VI
# Winter

When they were leaving the house, she stood ready and dressed in the doorway. Ian had become absorbed in Thomas Mann's *The Magic Mountain*. He stood in front of the bookcase in his boots with a scarf wrapped around his neck and shoulders. "We have to hurry," Elza said to him. "Yes, I'm coming," he nodded and turned the page. She stood silent in the doorway and looked at him. He kept reading. Focused. Under their feet a black hole opened up. A shaft. Life froze. No movement, no time. November. Sweat gushed from under their caps down their temples. Like blood after a shooting.

Elza returned home from the maze gradually. In stages. She emerged with effort from the accordion-like curtain. Endlessly repeating waves. She waited for the moment when the crashing of the shore overwhelmed the crashing of the waves. She inhaled. Her body was gradually reappearing at random moments, pieces of skin glowing like plankton. Bones biting through the frozen surface.

Kalisto Tanzi's labyrinth did not let you go easily: there was something for everyone in it.

(*Oh, little fairy*... For the fairy too.)

The mind also has its parts—neighborhoods, cities, districts, continents, amusement parks, Petržalka, Beverly Hills, Canada. Seas. Beaches—virgin with white sand, city beaches on the banks of highways. Much depends on the weather.

**Elza.** The Christmas season is always tough. Up to the surface float more and more misfits, masks, grotesque scenes. On the sidewalk in front of Café Hyena kneels an old woman vehemently writing something on the ground with chalk. Right under the feet of people hurrying by. It's dark. "Please give anything to help me surveil," she wrote in chalk slowly washed away under the footprints of others.

In the bus that goes to Petržalka, I listen to a slender man. He's sitting by the window, watching the scenery go past on the other side of the glass.

"I'm seeing this for the first time. I've never been here before. I'm here for the first time. Truly. And what's that?" he points to a temple-like building outside. "Tell me, what is that?" he says raising his voice and leaning over to the woman sitting next to him.

"KFC," she comments.

As they travel, Ian tells Elza how once, a long time ago, a girl made up a story about how she was pregnant by him. Now, when he comes to the town where she lives, he always bumps into her. He joins her, for a moment he's glad to see her, and then as she talks on and on he's flooded with an uncontrollable happiness. He turns off the sound and just keeps looking at her strange moving face and he's relieved that she's not his. That he doesn't have to drag her around with him all the time, like a horse through the whole town until they're so tired that they can go home again. Like a man walking through the city in winter. The chain on his leg slides around on the snow without clinking. The ball at the end of it flies around freely on the slippery patches, making joyful Christmasy ringing sounds. PING... PING... PINGPING... PING... PING... PING... PIGPING... PINGPINGPING... PING. Someone could confuse it with an orange or a set of jingle bells or register machine. Christmas is already approaching. Oh my God—he says again—Oh my God.


**Elza.** On the evening of December 23$^{rd}$ we go by tram to Café Hyena. Two girls are walking up and down the car with their heads bowed to the floor. They're searching. Something has fallen out of a pocket.

"What are you looking for, girls? What have you lost?" I ask them.

"A little white pill!" they laugh.

"What kind?"

"Don't ask."

"Oh, birth control."

"Uh-huh," murmur the people in the tram.

One of the girls sits down, takes off her boot and shakes it. Maybe the pill is in there. Maybe it fell into her shoe.

"So take the next one," a woman in a trench coat advises her.

"The one for tomorrow?"

"Yeah. That one."

"But what about tomorrow then?"

The tram floor is full of small stains, litter, dirt, stones, pieces of paper. The people on this line look intently under their feet. Even the sidewalk brings no relief.

In the café, next to Elza and Ian, sit a pair of young lovers (table no. 7).

They're smoking.

"I'm just asking whether you were really careful."

"I thought you were taking something."

"You haven't been careful this whole time?"

"You haven't been taking the pill this whole time? But you're a nurse! I thought every nurse took something."

"I brought you some gifts. To go under the tree," says a man with long hair (no. 4), pulling some items out of a bag.

"I took apart the survival knife. For Christmas you get fishing line and *you* get a compass. It's twenty years old and still works."

"Beautiful."

"I have two, I gave one to you and the second one I'll send to my daughter. In London. And now I have to go so I can get everything done."

"And what does she do? Your daughter who lives in London?"

"What else would she do? Same thing she does here. Takes drugs."

At table no. 8, two girls are smoking and drinking hot chocolate.

"So let him squirm, let him call you over and over again and don't answer the phone. Or, when he calls for the tenth time, answer the phone and tell him he's disturbing you."

"Yeah, but that's the problem—he doesn't call me at all," says the other girl, crying.

"He's doing it because he's jealous, it's clear. You know how guys are when they're jealous. Send him a text. I have a whole notebook full of texts. Some don't even say anything—they're neutral. For example, if you send him a text that says—Have you smiled yet today?—then it's impossible at that moment for him not to smile. You know?"

The customer at table no. 12 reaches his hand across the table and touches the gold necklace hanging on the neck of a young woman.

"Why are you wearing that relic of Christ?"

"You mean the cross? It has a nice shape. It's small and not very noticeable."

Both of them wet their lips on long-stemmed glasses.

Then, just as Elza and Ian have finished drinking their third glass of wine, they put down between them a plate of cheese with a sign on it reading, "Merry Christmas to our best customers." But it was one of a series of evenings when they weren't eating. "Wrap it up for us to give to the mice," Elza says to the waiter.

It's winter, December 23rd. In front of the café a vagrant mother hugs two children to her. She offers them cigarettes. A macho move instead of a coat. Steam and smoke rise from their mouths like columns to the sky. From time to time they cough. Deeply, as if they were about to begin a long speech.

# VII
## SECOND SUMMER

Elfman had a handsome but lined face. His features gave the impression they'd been etched by a tough fight with life. In reality, he had come by this face of an adventurer during a long battle with alcohol. Elfman's drinking had two phases: first he entertained his company, and then he threw up. He didn't much like the taste of alcohol, so he drank all kinds of fancy mixed crap or sweet dessert wines. He drank because alcohol made him charming and self-confident. Also because he liked to bring the glass to his mouth. He was enchanted by that movement of the arm that raises something to the lips. In reality, though, he was one of those people who didn't know how to drink. Every evening ended in nausea. Elfman had learned to deal with it elegantly—he had his methods. He held onto the sink with one hand and held his clothes to his body with the other. Sometimes though, he found himself in the wrong place at the wrong time, and then it happened that he threw up in a taxi and on Rebeka's dress too. She sat there next to his almost helpless body, the lap of her dress sprayed with his warm insides. Just like Jacqueline Kennedy.

She took Elfman tenderly in her arms. He was as light as a boy. The taxi driver took a breath as if to yell, but what he saw in the back seat reminded him of a Pietà. He helped the greenish-faced Maria carry the vomit-covered Jesus to bed. Rebeka offered the taxi driver a bowl full of fresh figs, took a bucket, and while he swallowed the last piece of fruit, she washed the inside of his car.

When she came back, she lay down in the other room. The view of Elfman's abandoned body had begun to terrify her. At once limp and stiff, soul-less, like a patient under anesthesia. They look so distant. You're almost sure that when they come to, they won't be themselves. She didn't want to touch Elfman anymore. Once when he came home very drunk before dawn, snorting, he leaned his forehead on the glass door and, convinced that he was in the bathroom, pissed right onto the telephone on the coffee table. Rebeka woke up to a sound similar to rain beating on the window. She could have stopped Elfman—he had only just started. She could have shouted at him. But she was afraid to intervene in the life of this desolate figure.

Then she remembered her mother's death. Mama had died at home in her bed. At the same moment, the bulb in the streetlamp in front of their house burst. Rebeka and her sister went to sleep. But in bed it occurred to her that, if they didn't intervene, her father would definitely lie down next to her mother on his side of the double bed. And they found him there too. "Dad, you can't sleep here, Mama's dead." "And where else should I sleep? This is my bed," said her father, pulling the covers up to his ears.

In the café, Elfman often expounded on the theory that the most difficult period of life is childhood. "When you realize how many traps are waiting for them, it's shocking how many people manage to survive it. Children have too much free time—they don't sit around in cafés, they don't hump and, instead of drinking, they spend time playing dangerous games in wild terrain, climbing trees, roofs, and posts." *Oh little fairy, if you only knew all the things I had to go through…*

From childhood, Elfman suffered from tics—something made him open his mouth wide from time to time, as if he wanted to scream, sing, or inhale sharply. His second tic was about throwing his head around. Like a horse when it snorts. The third one made him use dirty words: puke, puss, the shits, prick, cunt, fuck.

*(Oh little fairy, if you only knew all the things I had to fucking go through…)*

For this reason, he only got limited space in this book.

Elza's childhood nearly claimed two victims. (Summer holiday 1982.) Elfman squatted on the edge of a roof from which you could see the whole city. Elza came up behind him and pushed him toward the edge. Elfman used to terrorize girls in a similar way. But he did it as a trick. He lightly nudged their shoulders, but actually pulled them back toward him. Elza was not as clever.

A stronger Elza took seven-year-old acrobat Rebeka around on the handlebars of her bicycle. It was hot, they were going down a hill, and Rebeka couldn't keep her balance anymore. She begged Elza to stop. Elza laughed. She threw her head back, closed her eyes and sped up. Rebeka laughed too. With her last bit of strength—the last breath of friendship. When they fell, she flew over the front wheel. And boom, hit her blonde head on the asphalt. Elza's hands shook lightly on the handlebars. Dog days.

Elfman almost froze to death when he was a child. Father took him sledding on a Sunday afternoon. On the way to the hill, there were pubs. Father stopped in every one. "We'll rest for a minute, warm up our hands," he said each time. Everywhere he met friends, suddenly the whole world was full of them. One of them stuck his hand into a pocket inside his coat and pulled out a whistle. A gift for little Elfman. While Father drank, the boy blew on the whistle.

The friends clapped, and Father ordered him a red lemonade with a straw. Through the windows the sun quickly disappeared. Elfman's mouth began to hurt. Father's legs began to do the same. He couldn't get up. His friends took him out for some fresh air and put him in the sled. "Home," whispered Father with his last bit of strength. And Elfman hitched himself up to the sled. Pulling and crying, his toes stiff as wood inside his shoes submerged in water, disappearing like submarines.

It was snowing. Once in a while Elfman would check on his load—throwing his head around like a snorting horse. A golden horse. He was all white. In a turn his father fell out onto the road. He rolled. Elfman sat down in a hardened snowdrift. The whistle in his back pocket poked into him. He wanted to get up and pull it out. Then he forgot about it. He opened his mouth wide, as if he wanted to scream, sing, or take a big breath. But in the meantime the whistle had stopped bothering him. It had frozen to him.

They were awoken by the shouts of Grandma. She'd come looking for them.


**Elfman.** She caught father by the coat and leaned him up against a tree. She took off her gloves and rubbed his purple face with snow. Father opened his eyes. Grandma put her gloves back on and called out "box!" and punched father twice in the face. He started to laugh, and after a little while the laughter turned into vomiting.

Then she picked me up from the snowdrift and kissed me. The icy armor on my face (Tears & Snot, Inc.) cracked. Despite everything, my ears and nose remained in place. From my mouth came a stream of dirty words.

# VIII
## The Sea


"Well... now I really don't know which way to go..." Rebeka helplessly slowed down and peered questioningly at the signs at the intersection. The Quartet was on its way to the seaside.

"It's okay," said Ian. "Just keep going, according to *The Way of Not Knowing,* you'll reach enlightenment and save all living beings from their suffering."


**Rebeka.** I remember one day when I had that feeling. I was sitting in the car, we were stopped at an intersection at a red light. Suddenly a young man with a pistol was standing in front of my car. He was yelling. I didn't understand. He was standing with his legs apart in front of my car and aiming right at my face. It lasted quite a long time—maybe twenty seconds. Then he left. The light turned green. We started up. At home, wet laundry was waiting for me in the bathtub. And as I was wringing out those clothes, suddenly all of my restlessness melted away. I took a breath and sat down on the edge of the tub. The world was suddenly exactly as it should be. Everything fit together. And

I heard that sound and felt the roiling air—that bumping of things against the things next to them—when they fit into each other, when they even themselves out. My life adhered precisely to other lives. That feeling—it was the happiest I've ever felt. I wrung out my clothes hunched over the tub with the conviction that I would have that feeling forever, that I would never lose it, never forget, that I could call it up whenever I needed to. But it's not like that. I don't know how to get it back again. It's not possible. So how did you say that exactly... with those living beings?

Everyone enjoyed the sea. During their stay, Ian had vivid nightmares. Elza liked to swim, but went to bed early because the view of the sea at night terrified her. Rebeka always swam so far out that she barely made it back. She was drawn toward the horizon. (Its straight line.) Elfman hated the sea, sun, and sand. He constantly made this clear. This was added to his older tics. After two days he pulled his jeans on over his wet bathing suit on the beach and went to the stand to have a beer. Then he got in the car and headed for Vienna.

"Hello? Hello? Are you still lying around by that blue shit?" Elfman called them two days later from Bratislava.

We're in candyland. (Except for the cockroaches. Cockroaches? There are cockroaches in candyland? Yeah, and you should see them! There are cockroaches truly all over the world. In all worlds.)

Or, as Ian says, nobody tells the truth about their vacation. Nobody tells you how much they really suffered.

We're standing at the lookout point above the abyss. Parents are lifting children over the railing. Down below the sea is roaring. The children scream. The time will come for it all to turn around.

On Patmos, we found out about September 11, 2001, only on the 14th. The faces of islanders and tourists were submerged in newspapers. The surface (above them) closed up.

"It's really a bit too much—they've overdone it," commented the taxi driver who took us home from the Milan Rastislav Štefánik Airport. "If they blew up a bus or an embassy, I'd understand. That's okay. The Americans are up to their ears in it. Some two-story building or a train, that's one thing. But two skyscrapers, that's too much, they really went overboard."

"I always said that the Slovaks are a modern nation," said Ian, as he was stepping out of the car onto the rain-soaked ground.

**Elza.** After we came back from our vacation, I dreamt three nights in a row that I was by some beautiful water—by a lake, the sea, or on a beach. By an artificial sea that they built fifty kilometers from Berlin in an old hangar where they used to store Russian-made Tupolev airplanes. There are three suns shining constantly inside—one is rising, the second is exactly on the horizon, and the third is setting. They built an artificial sand beach there, filled the place with sea water, and people are sitting around on the beach, in the beachside bars, playing beach volleyball. Despite the heat, I can never go swimming. Either I'm in a huge rush to go somewhere, I'm in danger of losing my life, I'm looking for a beloved person, the beach is expecting to be bombed, or I can see under the surface of the sea that it's occupied. Full. There are shingled roofs of houses, smokestacks, tops of trees, electric power posts, roads, hills, concrete apartment buildings. Petržalka instead of Atlantis.

In the morning I go out onto the balcony. I try to calm myself down with breathing exercises—I smoke. Tranquility comes slowly.

I'll never get away from Petržalka. Petržalka is my yoga, my zen. I have to protect my beloved, who has gotten trapped in it. My beloved, wedged in by Petržalka. I have to continue on *The Way—Petržalka*, only then will I reach enlightenment and save all living beings from suffering.

"What, you think I shit money out of my ass?" the pancake asks his father on the other side of the wall. I leave the living room and look for a refuge from the voices in the bathroom. But here the shouts of the woman in love reach me. I have the feeling that they woke me up at night, took me out of my cell, and sat me down in front of a porno film. But not just any porno film. The kind of porno film where they shit and piss. Shit and piss on each other. History rushes through Petržalka. Ian and I live in the belly of Stalin just as Pinocchio did inside the whale. I hear every growl of the intestines.

Can you hear me? Hellooo? I'm thinking of the cable that people once had to lay on the ocean floor so that they could hear each other. In those days you had to yell into the telephone. Everyone could still imagine distance. Stalin worked with distances, made a planet earth out of his country, a state out of a city, a house out of an apartment, an apartment out of a room. A belly out of life. A universe out of a belly.

Petržalka. An advent calendar full of chocolates. Window after window, with a common backstage. Common spaces, a common, never-silent choir.

Elfman claims that the genius loci of Petržalka is in the fact that, in time, everyone here starts to feel like an asshole who never amounted to anything in life. A guy who couldn't take care of himself or his family. He didn't make it, couldn't climb up to the houses posing on the hills and peaks of the city. There, where his true home is. There, where people's backs are attached to heated car seats. Where they are surely looking for him and wondering why he's late for dinner.

Guests who came to Petržalka on a polite Sunday visit, pilgrims who had to travel through it, children who got stuck here, also succumbed to this feeling.

*(Some phenomena that we see in the world remind us of a situation where we look at Gorgon, but unfortunately, the sight of them doesn't turn us to stone.)*

**Elza.** In the beginning, when we were still just lovers and I would go to Petržalka for visits, I scared Ian several times. He bumped into me on his way from the bathroom to bed in the middle of the night and screamed in terror, as if he'd seen a ghost. Aghhhh. Aghhh—the scream of a man who sometimes sleeps alone and sometimes with his lover. A man used to an empty apartment at night. Full of dead parents and friends.

*Aghhhh*—he yelled at me—as if he'd finally tripped over that cadaver—he yelled at me like a ghost at a ghost: Gotcha! Let me finally see you. Face to face. I'm looking at you: horror at horror, let me see who you actually are in reality.

And then daytime always came and we laughed over that night terror. Even though it was clearer in the sunlight that that laughter was just another kind of aghhhh…

At night I awoke to a painful sore throat. It had ripped me out of a terrible dream. The pancakes had occupied the city. Dressed in black, their faces smooth-shaven and bleached—clean—as if washed by a heavy rain. Rebeka and I bump into each other downtown and try to escape. The road is lined with cafés, restaurants, and fitness clubs, turned temporarily into camps and dens full of people. They're crying. Their faces are covered with blood-soaked bandages. Most of them have no nose. Their teeth and mouths are beaten up and they have bandages on their throats. The pain radiates from them, their wounds flamboyantly colorful, glowing like Chinese lanterns. They're weeping and afraid. For a moment Rebeka and I rest by them and then run on. To the stop for bus number 104.

The whole way is lined with black-shirted men with porcelain-white faces and baseball bats in their hands. They smile at us. I'm trying to convince Rebeka to get off the bus with me just below the train station. She says no, that she's going to the end of the line in Oakville. So I get off without her. The bus takes her from me and I feel desperate that I haven't convinced her. I cry because I know that she'll step off the bus with that small foot of hers right into a sea of black-shirted men, among the baseball bats. I feel it by the name, by the word—Oakville.

I decide on my own journey. I don't know what to look for, a signal to guide me. There are two roads to my house. One leads through one tunnel and the other through two tunnels. From a distance I can already spot the black and white colors and bats by the tunnel. I sigh with relief when I manage to turn toward the two tunnels without being noticed. I stand in front of a big smiling group of the men and I can't understand how I could have forgotten that the two tunnel route is in the gypsy neighborhood. The pancakes are stretching and relaxing their muscles, looking at the gypsies, who are standing on the other side of the street. They are wiggling like children. Standing in place, squirming. My nose is hit by the scent of soap carried on the wind from the pancakes' faces. I go numb.

I wake up from the dream because of an unbearable sore throat. I look for a doctor. I sit in front of the ear, nose, and throat department and wait. I've come too early. The department is part of a hospital and they've just now finished their rounds. The waiting area is full of sick patients. Its walls glow from the flames of pain, wounds are lit and heating up. One girl with her face covered by a bandage weeps quietly. She weeps and weeps. She is soothed by a patient who's breathing through an opening in his throat and has a thick bandage around his neck and nose. A man with half of his face bandaged and a syringe with a line attached to it sticking out of a hole where his nose should be is pacing nervously up and down. I can imagine the wounds and their contours.

The weeping girl is still inconsolable. She can't catch her breath. She looks unwaveringly at me with black tear-filled eyes.

I go out onto the hospital grounds and stretch my legs in front of a bench. Right on top of a swastika painted on the sidewalk. I escape it with my eyes wide open. Like Rebeka's constant weeping in the waiting area.


When Ian left Petržalka for the first time and Elza was left in the apartment by herself, she suddenly realized how neglected the place was. She hadn't noticed before—for two whole years, since she'd come there, it hadn't bothered her that there was no running water in the kitchen, because when they needed to wash something, they did it in the bathroom. The first two years they only paid attention to each other. When Ian once hinted that they should go out for a walk together, she told him that for walks he should buy a dog.

The first thing she decided to get rid of was a pile of dirty laundry taking up half the bathroom. She gradually took the clothing and looked it over piece by piece—it took one whole day. By evening she began to reach the bottom of this mountain and toward dusk, she was more and more often seized by fear. She was scared that when she lifted the last stained piece of clothing from the floor, she would be surprised by a life that had been hiding at the bottom of the pile. A face. As repulsive as the layers of old, dirty, and smelly clothes that had already lost their color and shape and in time had become a heap. At the very bottom, under some brown pants, there was a pair of completely new women's boots.


When she was leaving the house in the evening, she was gradually greeted by the pancakes smoking by the entranceway.

"Hi."

"Hi."

"Hi."

She realized that she already really lived there. That she was at home. That she belonged to Petržalka. At night she was greeted by the shadows shifting their weight from foot to foot by the entranceway. She'd become one of the Petržalka backdrops. A piece of Petržalka. A piece of the Petržalka puzzle.

Amongst the concrete apartment buildings the click of heels dully resounds. The boots feel like they were made for her.

On Monday, Rebeka didn't show up for work. Even though it was pay day—the Trinity didn't get their stipend. At three in the morning Rebeka called for an ambulance. She said that a small and very fast dog had bitten her several times. In the face too.

The doctors decided that even though the wounds weren't visible, they would hospitalize Rebeka anyway. In the psychiatric ward.

# IX
## CarlSolomon*

*Carl Solomon is a man who Allen Ginsberg met at the looney bin in Rockland where they were both hospitalized and appears as a character in Ginsberg's poem, *Howl*.

**Elza.** I went to visit her in the hospital. Rebeka was my *CarlSolomon*. Ginsberg's first born lunatic from Rockland. He never stopped mentioning him. (*CarlSolomon! I'm with you in Rockland / where you're madder than I am/ I'm with you in Rockland / where you must feel very strange.*) *CarlSolomon*, I'm with you in Bratislava (*Where your condition has become serious and is reported on the radio*). *CarlSolomon*, I'm with you in the same stocking. A crazy stocking. A stocking full of holes. A stocking full of candy. Full of money.

**Rebeka to Elza.** When I was little, I really liked an ad for chicken soup. In it there was a giant yellow chicken. It seemed to me like that could be home. Inside such a roomy costume. I imagine myself sitting inside it quietly and for the first time, I am truly WITH MYSELF, home. The world around me pulses. I sit motionless, as if in the eye of a hurricane. In the beginning I look through the chicken's eyes and watch what's going on around me. I watch how people behave, enjoying myself and relaxing. Later I just cling to the inside of the costume. As the sun journeys toward the horizon, the walls change color. I'm safe.

**Elza.** I'm with you in the chicken, *CarlSolomon. Where we are great writers on the same dreadful typewriter.* I'm with you in the ad for soup. I'm with you in yourself, home, my little *CarlSolomon.*

We were in the café when Milka Vášáryová[3], Rebeka's favorite actress, sat down at the table next to us. She sat down there with two friends and they had strudel and coffee. Rebeka got nervous and started to look for a clean piece of paper so she could ask Milka for an autograph. She couldn't find one, just a box of medicine. "Hello Ms. Milka, would you please give me an autograph? But where? I don't have any paper, and nor do you. But you can do it here. You can sign my antidepressants…"

Tell me, Elza, would you ever have thought that would happen to me? Rebeka threw up her hands.

Of course, said Elza. Of course, *CarlSolomon.*

---

3    Milka Vášáryová is a very famous actress in Slovakia comparable in stature and elegance to Meryl Streep.

Ian remembers that when he was little, on their street a neighbor came back from the nuthouse after having electro-shock therapy. He came back home after two years. In a single night he cut down all the electric power posts on the street.

PING... PING... PINGPING... PING... PING... PING... PINGPING... PINGPINGPING... PING.

In Rockland there was also a small café. Patients and visitors met there. The doctors and attendants went there too. It was called Café Emotion. There was a little girl in a long dress here stirring her lemonade very fast with a straw, and she recalled: "I was swallowed up by sadness—saudade, tristeza, hünzün, emptiness, burn-out, rancor, barrenness—endless barrenness. Everywhere the eye may fall. A barrenness that wraps a person in white transparent slime so that they can more easily slide down the walls of hell. So that, without bumping into anyone, you can float, drift among people who are hurrying to work and among those who are meandering from shop to shop, and feel that their familiar routes that they take day in and day out like horses, like a merry-go-round, are the root system of hell, wider than the crown of heaven.

First it seized Mama. She lay in bed and covered her head with the quilt. When she had to, she got up, and walked by us at a safe distance. Silent. And then she returned to bed again and lay there with the covers over her head. When she spoke—to give some essential instructions for operation of the household—she never looked any of us in the eye or the face. She didn't raise her gaze higher than a meter from the ground. And we too preferred to stop looking at her. So that we wouldn't confuse her.

She didn't love us. I didn't love her. She lay in the next room and those closed doors drove me out of the house entirely. It wasn't okay anywhere. As if in one room there was always a monster.

I began to wonder what I'd done that was so horrible that Mama had changed like that. I guessed she wasn't happy with my lifestyle. Or she'd found the wrapping from a box of bonbons that I'd stuffed myself with without even offering her one. She'd discovered that her daughter was a miser and a glutton, and it had broken her heart completely, I thought, so I preferred to disappear from home for days at a time. I sat in pastry shops. Slept on benches. The belly of a house where I had floated around in whipped egg whites and Night&Day pudding had become filled with acid. The others avoided it too—my seven siblings and father. It came out that at one time or another all of us had secretly eaten an entire box of bonbons.

The gong sounded and on the café stage appeared a spotlight. The hobby of Doctor Typhoon, Head of Psychiatry at the clinic, was rock music. This nearly 70-year-old professor rode a motorcycle so that the wind would whistle in his ears, and also for the feeling that at any time he could crash and lose his life—literally kill himself.

It's daring to strive for a sunny economy. Sang Typhoon. The sun only gives and takes nothing. It gives and never dwindles. So lovely, oh so lovely—you are impressed by the sunny economy. Because I'm giving everything. And you nothing. When I look around. Behind us. We are just kitsch. We actually fit in. Setting behind the deer and the silver mountains like the evening sun. But I'm those places on your skin. That never tan. Sang

Typhoon. I'll let my hands melt into my own body at the sides. I keep the fast. Don't touch! Maintain the moon economy.

Rebeka watched Typhoon and her eyes turned into two small dogs. He's singing my heart, barked one over the other.

She loves him! Look at her, yelped Elfman. What a cliché. *Clichéshit.*

In addition to Rebeka, there were people at Rockland who'd been brought there by stories. Led by the hand. A man, who at 40 had decided to fulfill his parents' common dream—to see Canada—and bought them a two-week trip. And they got lost there in the woods and froze to death. In an embrace, at the foot of a tree. A snowdrift covered them up to their ears. (*Oh, little fairy...*) The son wanted as many of his parents' friends and acquaintances as possible to know about the sudden funeral, and so he put a notice in the newspaper. Some thieves saw it and robbed the parents' empty house, destroying the interior. It's so normal that the guy ended up in the looney bin.

There was also a woman there, who couldn't bear the fact that her husband had left her. So she took off into the woods to burn a bundle of love letters. Her husband had written them before they got married. The woman was the director of the nature reserve. When she burned the letters, a forest fire started. It lasted for two weeks and swallowed up the Australian National Forest. This woman was brought to Rockland by rituals. It's a diagnosis, said Dr. Typhoon. Ritual-seekers. They attract them from birth. In them they look for content that the rituals are supposed to accompany. But the rituals themselves don't contain it. These people get married because of the wedding ceremony and the rings. After a few years they take their rings off under dramatic circumstances (a storm, alcohol, pills) and then at every party show their colleagues how the ring has deformed their finger.


After his first visit to Rebeka in Rockland, Elfman left the city. Observers claim to have seen him walking toward the train station at dawn. He was mumbling something about puke and throwing his head around like a horse snorting.

No one knew where he'd gone. One could deduce, though, that it definitely wasn't to the sea. He wrote long letters to Rebeka in which he recalled all their lovely moments. He would never forget them. He would play them in his mind till the end of his life. Every letter ended with the words: And don't call me!


Rebeka didn't mind solitude. The only thing was that she stopped sleeping. "It's as if sleep wasn't necessary for a person who lives alone. I think that I've been sleeping till now so that I could get a rest from other people. From the others in the house. I closed my eyes, so that I could just be alone with myself."


When Elza was alone with Dr. Typhoon, she asked him whether he could figure out who had *CarlSolomon* in them and who didn't. He said that one can't tell by looking. Ian told her that he met *CarlSolomon* when he couldn't see. "You know, it wasn't that the world disappeared. It was me who disappeared. I wasn't there. In that darkness I ceased to exist."

The night before the operation on Ian's eyes, the nurse took him by the hand and led him to the telephone. The publisher was calling to say that Ian's new book was already at the printer. He was afraid, however, that in their haste they'd made a mistake on the title. He asked Ian whether it would bother him. If it came out with a different name. A little bit muddled. Six hours later they operated on Ian.

Elza stood in the hallway. With her back to the wall facing Ian's cheerful cries. She couldn't yet see the wheelchair they were pushing him in, but his joking met her halfway from afar.

And suddenly, they were all moving down the slippery white hallway in front of her—Ian's lively body and freshly bandaged eyes, his mouth grinding out word after word and the nurses laughing.

And Elza was frightened of the moment when Ian would be lying in bed and, instead of a tongue pushing off quickly from the teeth and palate, the sharp paddles of a mill would start churning behind his high forehead. The wings of a machine following patches and spirals of radiant pulsing colors that he would have to look at. Like a boy who, during after-lunch nap time, entertained himself by pushing down on his eyelids with his fingers. Harder and harder.

According to Dr. Typhoon, *CarlSolomon* emerges mostly as an embryo within an embryo. And then gradually grows and matures until it decides it is grown up and becomes independent. That's when a person goes crazy.

On Sunday, Rebeka unexpectedly fell into a deep sleep. On the pillow next to her head lay Elfman's cap. In the role of a teddy bear. Both will sleep until the end of this story.

**Elza.** I'm walking up the hill above Rockland. It's a warm day. I look down from the foot of the hill at the playground. The CarlSolomons are playing soccer. Their shouts rise to the sky. Every player has their own ball.

Dr. Typhoon is standing on the sidelines singing: And I think about my deaf and dumb parents, how they reproached me for something, how they argued with me. And passionately educated me. Like two water mills. Moving their hands like paddles. Like birds batting their wings, like a hand with a feather duster sticking without context out of a window on the sixth floor: how their hands in sign language whipped up the dust from the tops and peaks of the wardrobes and secretaries and from the round face of the old globe with its obsolete political divisions of the world. And how during the arguments their faces became more and more ashen with dust. And how crystals of salt floated around the kitchen like in the sea. And in me water rose steeply, first to the mouth and then to the nose. Wavy water, which comprises three quarters of a human being.

The first steps toward Rockland, according to Dr. Typhoon, must be sought in childhood.

# X
# Childhood

**Elza.** My childhood was marked by socialist materialism. That is, until the arrival of the new girl. She moved to Waldemar Street when I was twelve. Her father was a socialist diplomat. She had completely different toys than I. I had Slovak dolls in folk costumes and one wooden one—from Romania—which my father had brought from a business trip as proof that in Romania they truly had nothing. The new girl had Monchhichi and Barbie, listened to Limahl, Duran Duran, Nena, and Nina Hagen, and cut pictures out of *Bravo* magazine. Every night she dreamed the same dream: in it she was driving the tram on the track from Bratislava to Vienna.[4]

I liked Monchhichi best of all. I asked my parents to buy me a Monchhichi somewhere. In our shops they didn't have them and my father brought me some stupid mole as a substitute. Mama wrote one at a time to all our relatives and friends who had emigrated and lived in the West. She asked them for God's

---

4 At that time, it wasn't possible for people to go from Bratislava to Vienna. Although the distance between the two capital cities is only 60 kilometers, the border between communist Slovakia and capitalist Austria was closed.

sake to send me a Monchhichi. She wrote them that it was top priority. (So when will it be that day already? When will I get it? When will you give it to me?)

We were just picking grapes in the garden when the postman brought a package. Beneath my feet the earth suddenly began to turn faster and faster. In the package was a Monchhichi. My life could now go on, my body grow, my mind develop. I knew that I would live.

(I always woke up earlier than Ian. I watched at his sleeping, sometimes calm, sometimes pucker faced. In the morning, I always had the feeling that Ian was my child. Except that I don't get why he was born to me with a mustache and beard already. Such an extremely late-term baby. With a nose like a Monchhichi doll. A monkey that caused all socialist children to endlessly bug their parents.)

Aunt Milka sent me a Monchhichi. A friend of my mother's who had emigrated to Canada. She lived in an area where it was mostly around minus 40 degrees, and taught at a school for Inuit children.

In '68, she was supposed to marry a Viennese man. At home there was no one holding her back, her mother had died when she was still a child, her father had a new wife. Milka's first marriage with an animal tamer in the circus fell apart like the teeth of an old clown. She packed up everything she had, including the down quilts, and headed for Vienna. But no one was waiting for her there. Milka decided that since she had packed so thoroughly, she wouldn't go home again. She went to the camp for emigrants and from there to Canada. Twenty years later, she would send me a Monchhichi from there.

Some places on earth are cursed. For example, Moscow. Or Piešt'any. In Piešt'any my brother nearly died. We had gone there on vacation. Mama was in the spa for treatment there and we wanted to be with her. Daddy got us a rental apartment—one big room for the four of us at the house of two older people who could have been around fifty years old, but to me at five, they looked like grandma and grandpa.

The first day, when we arrive in Piešt'any, we all go together to the covered swimming pool. At five, I am unbelievably excited every time we go to a swimming pool, because—in contrast to my brother who is two years older—I know how to swim. Even though I must admit that I stay above water best when I swim on my back. My brother would just tread water and desperately cling to the side of the pool, his lips turning blue as if he wanted to blend in with the color of the water. A non-swimmer's camouflage.

Whenever I swim near him, he lets go of the edge of the pool with one hand and pushes my unsuspecting head, as it looks to the ceiling, down underwater. Water gets in my eyes and nose. I choke for a moment. My brother laughs for a long time. Blue laughter. That's what I get for being the first one who can keep their head above water. I resolve not to speak to my brother the whole time we're in Piešt'any.

When we come home, the old woman we are staying with gives me a necklace with a pendant. The pendant is a green spider with a red glass belly. For a moment my parents protest this gift. But it doesn't help. My brother likes the spider a lot. When the old woman leaves our room, my parents tell me not to address her in the informal, but in the formal. I don't understand this at all, but I decide to try. I've already got the chain with the spider around my neck.

When I wake up, the second day in Piešt'any begins with

breakfast at the milk bar. Sweet pastries, butter, jam, and warm cocoa. I'm in seventh heaven. I play with the new spider. The red belly brings him to life in the morning light. The same as my brother's cheeks. He slurps cocoa while his eyes shine. I'm already talking to him too. My anger never lasts long, there's no reason for revenge.

After breakfast, we stroll through the city. It's full of Arabs with turbans on their heads and lots of wide open spaces with planted flowers. But we have to interrupt our walk. My brother doesn't feel well. He's vomiting cocoa and pastries. We go home. The old man and woman are surprised that we've come in so quickly from outside on such a beautiful day. My parents explain to them that my brother has suddenly fallen ill. The old man strokes my brother's face. The old woman gives me a riddle: do you know how to get through a gateless gate?

My brother's fever rises. We sit quietly at the table—me, Mama, and Daddy. My brother falls asleep in bed. Then suddenly he wakes up and begins to yell: Mama! Mama! I'm deaf! I've gone deaf! Mama lies down next to him and tries to explain that his ears are blocked from the fever, but he doesn't hear her.

My father picks my brother up in his arms from the bed and we go to the emergency room. We stand in a narrow hallway waiting area—only now do I notice how my brother's legs have gotten longer. They're long and swing woodenly as they hang from my father's arms—just like the legs of a Pinocchio doll. Pinocchio, who went deaf in Piešt'any this evening. (*Oh little fairy, if only you knew...*)

I resolve never to get angry at him again when he pushes my head underwater while we're swimming. When I look at his burning face, for the first time I doubt the virtue of the spider with the fiery belly that I've had around my neck since arriving in Piešt'any.

In the fall, the time came when I stopped going straight home from school. Some of my classmates had turned into pals, fellow pilgrims, nomads. Best-friend love had broken out. It was fulfilled in the act of seeing each other off. It reflected in fresh puddles where golden leaves floated. Here and there, like in an aquarium. Unable to interrupt trusting conversations and say goodbye, we shared each other's way. From home to home. Like little dogs that hesitate in the middle of the street between two masters. (Cars honking.)

The red thread of intimate dialogue led through a labyrinth of new neighborhoods. The city had grown. Together we explored new areas, streets, stairways, gates. With every new rapprochement, the labyrinth got larger. We searched for detours.


We did not cross the river, though.


When I'm 13, I convince my parents to take the whole family on a vacation to Yugoslavia. I use the argument that I'm a noble child, who longs for the sea, but in reality, I want to go to Yugoslavia to buy *Bravo* magazine. (Who would travel so far for some blue shit anyway?)


Our dog was a small dachshund with German predecessors. Mostly purebreds. Mama called him Aladar. In time, however, his Nazi-Hitleresque nature rose more and more strongly to the surface. He bit every member of the family. He was treacherous—first he wagged his tail, wanting to play and be cuddled, and when someone took him in their arms, he attacked. He preferred to bite directly in the face. Mama forgave him everything.

He charmed her with his beauty. With his fur that shined golden in the sun, and his tail, which he carried like a blond flag. With his pretty face. Aladar sat on her knees when she watched television. He would suddenly start growling at her hand. "Oh, Aladar, you don't like my left hand?" asked Mama and hid her hand behind her back. Aladar slept next to her in the bed. In the beginning, he lay by her feet, then he found his place on the pillow. He went to bed earlier than Mama and always lay down like a noodle across the whole pillow. When he was thirteen years old, he got sick. At night he jumped onto the dining table and howled at the darkened crystal chandelier. In the end, he pissed on the tablecloth. Mama got sick and for days he didn't let anyone into her room. I remembered how once, when we all proudly went as a family to a dog show, he bit a judge in the cheek.

Aladar's illness got worse—he dragged his legs behind him, dribbled urine everywhere he went, and was tortured by terrible hunger. That was the only way to kill him. He couldn't resist a pot full of beef. That morning he got into my parents' room and intentionally pissed on my father's side of the bed. I decide to kill the dog and thus save all living beings from suffering. I put on some thick worker's clothes and gloves. His bowl of food I put into a big bag with a zipper. I lured him into it. The dog barked, howled, and growled. It was clear to him that I was abusing his wolf-hunger, his insatiability, in order to murder him. A couple of times, half his body was already inside the bag, but when he began to growl, I couldn't finish the job. I burst into tears. "Aladar, please, go inside. Please." I cried, the dog howling. We looked each other in the eye, showed each other our teeth—it was clear that one of us was not going to come out alive. Finally, I managed to shove his wiggling little head into the bag and zip it up.

In my worker's garb, I walked down the street to the veterinarian's office. In the bag, the whimpering dog squirmed helplessly. I knew that I would never go back home with him again.

I'd rather die. I would go to the vet and have him put down, and if the vet wasn't there, I'd go to the Old Bridge and throw the bag into the Danube.

At the vet's they'd give him an injection. Aladar would piss for the last time, this time on my worker's outfit, because when they did it, I would be holding him in my arms (the vet would tie his mouth shut beforehand). The vet would not forget to tell me that the fact that Aladar had bitten and attacked everyone was our fault, because "bad dogs don't exist, only bad owners." Then I would go home, up the river bank with an empty bag, in urine-soaked clothes. It wouldn't bother me at all—I'd be happy with this last dose of dog pee and my coat would pleasantly stick to my naked body like prima materia.

At home I would take the faces of the saved beings into the palms of my hands.


And if there's no one at the vet's, I'll go to the Old Bridge. I'll wait until there's no one around and I'll throw the bag with the dog into the Danube. Then I'll take such a deep breath that my lungs will fill half my body and reach all the way to my sex. A proud, young executioner. I'll walk over to Petržalka.

# XI
## Youth

When Elza was fifteen, she started going to the Puddle Bar. There everyone called her Polly. Polly, Polystyrene, Polynora, Polyndra, Polichka. Bookshelf Polly would probably have been the most accurate, because Polly was a pathologically prolific reader. For entire days, while eating and during conversations with people, she was always simultaneously reading something.

"Don't read while you're talking to me, Polly! Stop already!" shouted her friend Dennis whenever he was talking about his worries about their relationship and she was saying: uh-huh, uh-huhhhh. Her eyes would wander then, since she couldn't openly keep them trained on a book. So that she wouldn't seem too arrogant, she would at least run her gaze up and down the names of the records stacked on top of each other in the tall bookshelf.

Polly was always confused by Dennis's concerns. She liked his voice and face, his apartment full of books, which his father had once systematically taken and made into a beautiful and almost complete library. But she knew that on her journey awaited other apartments with almost complete libraries and with exactly those titles that were missing from Dennis's father's library.

Elza got the nickname Polly because at the Puddle, always after 10 p.m. and two bottles of red wine, she monotonously returned to her favorite subject of how monogamy is a cliché, which is just systematically instilled in us. We're like those children in the Huxley book where the newborns are gathered together in big rooms and made to listen for hours to recorded phrases like: This and that are good. This and that are bad. And those children, when they grow up, simply know that this and that are good and this and that are the opposite. And they think that they must have had it instilled in them by God or by themselves, by their nature, their essence, that it very simply just is the truth. It doesn't occur to them that it's nothing more than nonsense, crap that they've poured into their heads. Polly started on this monologue after ten o' clock in the evening, standing on a barstool. "And they've brainwashed us on monogamy. A woman with several lovers can only be: A) a whore; or B) an artist."

"Okay, Polly, don't go on about it so much, here we've all adopted polygamy," said her friends, quieting her.

"You haven't adopted shit!" yelled Poly at them and, furious, left for the bathroom. In the doorway she bumped into her best friend, the Englishman. Dominik, who'd been nicknamed the Englishman in the bar, was tall, burly, a bit English-style ugly and after ten o' clock and five pure malt Glenfiddichs, his sentences always began with *London*. The Englishman had lived half a year in London. Before that, in Bratislava, and before that, in a little village. When he went from the village to Bratislava, he said: "Oh God! God! Bratislava, this is the life! This is fun!"

Now he turns up his nose. "You can't even take a walk here, because you get to the other side of the city in ten minutes. And then what? Go around again?"

The Chinese girl Figu-Li[5] walked into the bar. She's a writer and, unlike the others, is well-known. She often uses culinary and fashion metaphors. For example: Words find their own garb, cut, and size. Then you just have to steam them in a covered pot for a while so that the flavor intensifies.

Figu-Li is in love with the Englishman and after ten, she always threatens to write a novel about the two of them. She'll never write it, though, because she's afraid her husband Wong would figure out that the novel and the love story in it aren't made up. Even though at the top of every page would be the words: *these characters exist only in the author's imagination.*

So she prefers to write novels where all the male characters are like fish that gradually swim into one whale—and that whale is Wong.


Polly and Dennis sat in the café on the boat. It was one of those times when once again she realized that there was a river flowing through the city. It suddenly became a priority for her during that summer and she always tried to be close to it. That's why she'd come to love even this bad café. It had just stopped raining and so they were the first on the boat. The waiter had to wipe off the wet chairs for them. Then a trio boarded the boat—an older woman, younger woman, and a little boy. They sat down at the table next to Polly and Dennis. And they began to interest Polly more than the river.

The little boy shot away from the table straight toward two plastic horses, which were on the prow of the boat to entertain children. One gold horse and one white one.

"They're wet, those horses," the older woman shouted at him, but then took no more notice of him because she and the younger woman started talking in muted voices about

---

5   A reference to well-known Slovak writer Margita Figuli.

something very important. Polly had already figured out that they were mother and daughter and hadn't seen each other in a very long time.

In the meantime, the boy had taken off his sweater and was wiping the rainwater off the horses slowly and thoroughly, with the true love of a real jockey. Then he took turns rocking on each of them and every few minutes jumped off and ran to the two women who were deep in conversation. He babbled something. Polly always understood only a few words from his excited talk: *My horsies... I'll gather some straw here... give them the straw... they eat straw.* When he understood that the women weren't paying attention to him, he began to shout: Look! Horsies! Look!

"Can't you see we're talking? Why are you shouting?" snapped the two angry women, who had completely forgotten that he was a child, and he belonged to them, or that at least they had gotten on the boat with him.

At that moment, another family came on deck—a man, woman, and two children—a bit older than the little jockey boy. The girl tore away from her father and ran toward one of the horses. She got on. The jockey froze. The muscles in his youthful face stiffened. But one of the horses remained free. "Run! Peter! Run! Come quick and get on the other horse!" the girl shouted to her brother, giving a challenging look to the jockey, who was much closer to the horse than her brother, but who had been riveted to the floor by her shouts. "Run, Peter! Before someone else gets on him!" The brother shuffled slowly over and clumsily got on the horse. The jockey's lips began to move very quickly. At first, Polly understood only a psalm from that quick speech: *my horsies, my horsies,* and then only—*they're not good horsies anyway, they're not real, they're fake, fake horsies.*

Dennis coaxed Polly off the boat. He said that when he'd noticed that mentally retarded boy dancing around the rocking horses and babbling, he'd gotten sick to his stomach.

They bumped into the two women and boy again. He wasn't

retarded. He was standing by a small but deep puddle, looking intently into it. He was warning the women not to get close to the edge. So that they wouldn't step in it. Why? The women asked him.

"Because there's a big catfish in it," said the fisher-boy. "A giant catfish."

"In such a small puddle there can't be a giant catfish," commented Dennis.

The boy looked at him from one eye to the other, a look full of terrible knowing, and slowly, with self-assurance, he said: "He's coiled up."

The boy was named Ian. He was seven years old, Polly fifteen. In twelve years they would see each other again at Café Hyena and that very evening would sleep together in Petržalka. That night (after 10:00 p.m.), Elza would stop spreading the notion of polygamy and obsessively reading.

And Ian would begin to grow old seven times faster than usual.

# XII
## The End
## (of childhood and youth)


Although during my life I have written under various pseud-
onyms (Elza, Rebeka, Ian, Elfman, Kalisto Tanzi, Wolfgang,
Sang-Fun, Typhoon, Polly, CarlSolomon), I still remember what
I was always called: "Play, Spot!"

Like the very fast and small dog. Or a juke box.

(PING… PING… PINGPING… PINGPINGPING…
PING.)

# XIII
## Seeing People Off

The boy draws a route on the map. In the evening he'll go to the movies with a girl. He is looking for the longest way from the cinema to the girl's home. The longest loop. A crazy zig-zag. A strange labyrinth.

When Mama began to die, Ian chose the same path.


**Elza.** I'm sitting on the bus and need to pee. It's a long way. Without a break. Without stops. Without any relief. I've needed to pee like this for hours, so badly that I'm beginning to feel like inside, instead of a heart, brain, and blood, all I have is urine. I can't ask the driver to stop. The aisle is full of desperate standing passengers. I would have to jump from one head to the next to get out. Helpless, I think of those beings who had to pee for hours, so badly that instead of curling brain tissue and blood, they had urine and the urine overflowed into their heart and through their veins and became their pulse, and they traveled, tense and without a word in the trains and under truck beds, and I think about prisoners, hostages in the Russian musical theater who relieved themselves among the seats, and about that philosopher who was embarrassed to interrupt a discussion and leave the table to go to the bathroom until, in the middle of the feast, right in the middle of a thought, his bladder burst.

About that German woman who came into the tourist bathroom on the cliff of the Portuguese shoreline and went from door to door, banging with her fists and shouting "Hilfe! Hilfe!" And outside her German husband was walking around pretending that he didn't know her and was there totally by chance.

And about Rebeka when she was on that trip to Paris, holding it and holding it until her teeth began to quietly chatter and she felt like she was being poisoned. Until Elfman made her drop her pants right in the middle of a Parisian boulevard full of people because he couldn't listen to that chattering anymore, and he stood over her, yelling: "Piss for God's sake! Take a piss, sweetie!" And she, delirious for a moment, actually forgot about the world and the people around her.

And I'm thinking about Ian's mama, whose long illness began with her not being able to find the bathroom anymore, although she knew she should still be looking for it. That you can't just pee anywhere.

And at night she peed into her walking shoes.

With such precision!


**Elza to Ian.** And I'm thinking about how we used to live in a rental apartment owned by Doña Maria Da Luz. We lived in the same apartment with her—she was the boss. And after we made love, I would go and wash the dishes and you would sleep. And then you would run to the bathroom.

It was locked. The boss lady was sitting on the toilet. Helpless, you ran to me and pushed me and the dishes aside a little bit and pissed. In a big arch, over the cups and plates, directly into the drain. And I felt like Doña Maria was going to open the door, I was scared that she'd come into the kitchen. And you just pissed and pissed. As if it had no end, as if you were suddenly bottomless and couldn't get enough of that kitchen freedom. And then without a word, you left. Free and proud as a young wolf. From the sink (like from your fur) hot steam rose.

And I think of children whose beds are still covered with plastic in adulthood. Of a wet circle on the pants of a smiling drunk— a mandala shimmering in the first rays of the morning sun.

I think of Ian, who was standing in the pub's cement yard helplessly rattling the handle on the locked door of the outhouse. Of the yard-owner's cry from the pub door. "What are you doing here? For God's sake!"

"Can't you see I'm pissing. I'm pissing, so don't yell at me. There's no stopping it."

A family barricade. It's five in the morning, I'm sitting on the carpet in front of the door, crying. On the floor on the other side of the door sits Ian's mama. One can't get in. Or get out. Family fortress. Barricade. Wall.

I'm helping Ian put Mama in bed. She is so small and dried out. We've been seeing her off for a while now. Ian examines her bedsores. Her feet are purple, filled with dark blood. I remember when years ago she began to forget and still realized it—she said that the forgetting was certainly from waking up very early as a child and trudging a long way to school. She would join the workers in the dark. She could hardly keep up with them. And it was worst in winter. That's why she can't remember anything now, she said. Every time I looked at her blood-filled feet I had the feeling that every night while we were asleep, she must have walked that long and difficult road in the dark and joined the workers on their way to work again.

Does this tram go downtown?
  And where should it go?
  Downtown.
  But where downtown?
  To the church.
  Which church?
  On the square.
  The woman who wants to go to the church doesn't understand the people's advice. They're confusing her, especially with the landmarks, street names, squares, everything specific and precise. An older man tries to help her by giving her the old names of places from years back. Do you need to get to Stalin, madam? To Stalin Square?

Mama also began by forgetting the names of the streets. Followed by the names of her children and husband. I never had children, she said. Then she stopped understanding the meanings of words. At night through the door I would tensely listen as she recited Hail Mary. Exactly, without mistakes, word by word.

Despite the fact that she didn't understand the words anymore. She used them randomly. According to some unknown key. She repeated them like a muezzin's call. (*Father is bad, swine*—she would say when she felt lonely. *Miserable idiots, dummies*—she would shout angrily. *Kenyérke*[6]. *Little cakes and sauces*—that's what she called hunger. *Mrs. Doctorkova* was someone who would make her healthy again. Or at least was supposed to.)


Mama didn't remember anymore that Ian was her son. But a new memory took shape in her. Ian was a person who took care of her. "You are the best." She hugged him when he came into her room. "Miserable idiots, miserable idiots," she whispered behind the door when he left. "You are the best." She stroked Elza's hair. "Dummy, dummy," she repeated angrily, when she was left alone.


Elza placed some mashed potatoes with finely chopped white meat in it on the table in front of Mama. Mama only liked lively colors, she didn't trust darkly colored foods. She slowly ran the fork over the surface of the mash. Ian brought the roasting pan with the chicken and put it down in the middle of the table. Mama longingly looked at the piece of roasted meat. Suddenly, she had recognized the true, un-degenerated form of food. She still remembered how temptation was supposed to look. "*Kenyérke*," she said. "You have the same thing, Mama," explained Elza. "It's just cut up small so that you can swallow it more easily." But Mama couldn't take her eyes off the roasted meat. After a moment she pressed her lips together and pushed the plate of mashed potatoes away. "I'll give you some of it, Mama. But you won't eat it. Will you eat it?" Elza cut a piece of meat and put it on Mama's plate. Mama looked at the chicken with satisfaction. After a while though, she got nervous. She didn't know where to begin. Fear was encroaching. She quickly

---

6   "Kenyérke"—a diminutive of the word for *bread* in Hungarian

rose from the table and locked herself in her room away from the roasted chicken leg.

Mama was a big television watcher. When she was still healthy, she used to watch television every night—the news and then some drama or series. She didn't even want to travel because she claimed that in a foreign country she would miss the Slovak television shows. She knew the names of all the Slovak actors. (*This film must by very old because Mistrík[7] looks so young in it.*)

When she got sick, the television began to frighten her—she felt like the actors were directly addressing her. As if those people from the screen always wanted something from her. "I have enough problems of my own," Mama said, pushing them away. The only thing she could watch in the end was Commissar Derrick[8]. The last things that were familiar to her on television were his kind and bulging eyes.

Mama sat in the garden and watched Ian cutting the grass. "Agile," she wanted to say with admiration. "Fragile," she said instead.

As for visitors, at first Mama looked forward to having people in the house. They interested her, she wanted to be with them in the same room. After a while, though, she began to fear them. Especially if they talked a lot or laughed loudly. They were too

---

7    Ivan Mistrík was a very famous actor in Slovakia comparable in stature and elegance to Paul Newman.

8    *Derrick* is a German television crime series made between 1974 and 1998. The main character, an investigator from the homicide section, was played by Horst Tappert, an actor known for his bulging eyes.

much of a mouthful for her. She would slowly rise from her chair and try to leave without being noticed. She would slip into her room, but not lock the door. After a while, she'd tiptoe back to it. She'd stand behind the slightly open door and watch the people in the room through the narrow crack. Her presence was only betrayed by a quiet, terrified whispering, which she couldn't contain.

Ian knew this position behind the cracked-open door well. As a child he'd often stood there in his pajamas, trying to secretly watch the television in the other room. Although his parents sat with their backs to him, they knew he was there without turning around.

Ian looks at his face in the mirror and says that he sees Mama. "The older I am, the more I resemble her. The more I look like her. I look at myself and see her face. Still healthy."

Some words escaped harm. Even if Mama forgot that she had children and their names didn't mean anything to her, she didn't forget about Mrs. Doctorkova, although she didn't actually exist.

Of her three children, she remembered her son in America the longest. She waited for him to save her from the other children who'd remained at home and become *dummies* and *miserable idiots*.

She became a childless woman who'd never been married. From childhood, she remembered only her father, who had left the family when she was little. She periodically waited for him and hoped he would take her home, and cursed him, saying he was a bastard. She asked Ian every morning how she'd gotten there and with whom. How long would she need to stay?

She mentioned *kenyérkes, sauces,* and *little cakes* because she was constantly hungry. She suffered because she'd forgotten how to swallow. She was afraid to put something in her mouth. She didn't know what she would do with it in there. The food grew in her mouth. She couldn't breathe. Elza fed her in spoonfuls. Mama pressed her lips together. Locked her mouth shut.

In the morning, she tenderly took Ian's face in her hands. "You have a beautiful beard," she said passionately. Elza remembered the white beard of Walt Whitman. She'd read about how it looked good enough to eat. "Okay, Mama, let the man be… Come on, let's go into the living room."

"Those *sauces,* Mama must have gotten that from me," said Ian to Elza. "When I was a kid, I was always bugging her that I wanted to eat sauce with everything. Sauce, sauce—I used to bang the spoon on the table."

Mama accepted fewer and fewer spoonfuls. Elza and her man suspected she would die of hunger. "Kenyérke," she repeated, sitting at the table. "Would you really like a kenyérke, Mama? I'll bring you one." Elza put a slice of bread in Mama's hand. "They didn't give me a kenyérke," Mama repeated and peered fearfully at the bread in her hands. With one hand she smoothed the white tablecloth, in the other she held the bread and talked endlessly about kenyérkes. Elza sat at the head of the table. Weeping.

One night, Mama forgot about her teeth. She had taken out her false teeth the evening before, and when she woke up in the morning it seemed impossible that they had anything to do with her. The idea of putting those teeth in her mouth terrified her. Something so big, sharp, and hard did not belong in a mouth. What would happen to her tongue? How would she breathe then? She refused to even look at them. She hid them instead. Under the pillow, on top of the cupboard, in the vase.

It took Elza hours to put them back in her mouth. (*Open your mouth and put your teeth in! Put your teeth in, Mama. You have to put them in your mouth. Don't worry, Mama, they're your teeth. Put them in your mouth.*) Those were the teeth days, the dental bridge days. She would stand constantly in front of Mama with the teeth in her hand. She had to block her way, follow her around—otherwise she would never put them in her mouth again. Her lips would disappear. Her mouth would go away, as if something had devoured it. (Her cheeks?) Her face would turn into a sink-hole. A labyrinth.


Elza would run around the apartment after toothless Mama, constantly offering her the teeth. She clutched the teeth tensely in her hand. Mama wept from fear. Ian plugged his ears. Elza ran out into the yard, helplessly clenching her fists, fingers curled over bitten-up palms.


**Elza.** Mama falls asleep and we go into the room next to hers. We watch television. A film where people are gradually eaten by dinosaurs.

"Haven't we seen this already?" I ask.

"Not this one," says Ian.

"But I feel like we have, we've already seen it."

"Definitely not."

I rely on Ian to know. But after a half hour I fall back into doubt.

"But I actually remember this scene."

"Aha, I guess we've seen it," Ian finally admits.

The horrific scenes in the film intensify. We go quiet. When the dinosaur crushes the leg of a young woman scientist between his teeth, I yell: "Agh!"

"Oh come on, Elza, it's just a film! Although I also don't get how they could have lost all their weapons so fast!" Ian says, upset when the dinosaurs start chasing the whole group of explorers. When one of them trips, Ian yells.

"Should I change the channel?" I ask.

"No, but turn it down, please. They always scream so loud in those American films."

I went into the kitchen and began to read a book. All happy stories. The fight between humans and monsters accompanied by Ian's shouts kept tearing me away from my reading. The last story was unexpectedly long and sad. I turned off the light and fell asleep a moment after Ian. When we got up in the morning, Mama was already dead.

## XIV
## SECOND WINTER

**Elza.** Brown city snow. Baked into mounds of lumpy ice. I walk through the streets, tripping over gray bony faces full of holes and hollows. The beleaguered face of snow in the city. My body stops functioning on auto-pilot, all by itself. The puppet strings that move the limbs, other times so taut, strained, are sprawled on the floor, fuzzing up together, tangling underfoot. It takes an eternity for the leg to finally bend at the knee, the body to fold at the waist, the fingers on the hand to move. My face tries to huddle together with those on the ground. The features react to gravity. The view is exhausting. Ian and I hold hands with difficulty. The only thing we like to talk about is Mama's death. We remember her dying as if we were putting icicle-charged electrodes to our wilted, lumpy temples.

*(Oh, CarlSolomon…)*

In the evening we eat meat and wash it down with African wine. In quantities so big as if to poison ourselves. I watch my body changing. In some places the bones are disappearing, in others humps and knobs emerging.

African wine is like the African sun. It takes everything you've got.

Christ once said that he who does not rise from the dead during life can absolutely forget about it after death.

In the movie theater they're playing Fellini's *La Dolce Vita*. There are flashing masks, monsters, vaginas on high heels. Italian children see the Madonna in every corner. An excited female voice breaks into the Italian soundtrack from the back rows of the theater: I know you. You're from Piešťany. Stop burning me! We don't do that here! Stupid Piestanians, they're burning my knee with a laser!

Immediately following there is movement in the back. The woman pushes her way past the sitting viewers. Give my regards to Piešťany! she shouts. She stays standing until the film ends. She's wearing a puffy jacket—like the Michelin man. From time to time she moves her arms back and forth by her body. The jacket whistles with each movement. Crackles like wood in a fire. Flares behind our heads.

*(Ach, CarlSolomon, I'm with you in Piešťany!)*

When Elza asked Ian why she had constantly felt like crying for three days, he said, because she's grown up. Life isn't only about putting on a smile, he smiled. The crying passed.

The woman in the tram pulled a seated hood toward her. From it emerged the head of a black-haired boy.

"Excuse me, where is the police station in this city? I need to go to the police. I saw something," said the woman.

"The police?" I don't know. Really. I'm actually not from here," stammered the boy.

"You either? This is weird! Is there anyone here who's actually from here?"

On Thursday, Ian and Elza received a Christmas card from Elfman. The envelope was covered with bells and stars. In the place where the return address should be was a stamp: Wolfgang's Animals. And *don't call me!* someone had written by hand.

Ian's tooth hurt. He paced up and down the apartment all night. Once in a while he would lie down next to Elza only to find that he couldn't stay lying down. The pain didn't allow him to change from a vertical position. It kept him upright with his feet on the ground, his head just below the ceiling (like a balloon full of gas). Whenever Elza woke up, she saw his back, face, the crown of his head—everything fused together in an aura of pain—dark and sharp like metal shavings gathered around a magnet.

The dentist gave him an injection, and while it took effect, they talked. They discussed politics until Ian's mouth got completely numb. "It was a baby tooth," said Ian to Elza and stuck the tooth in his pocket.

Death doesn't exist, repeated Elza.

When Elza and Ian got off the elevator on their floor, in the dark hallway a radiant neighbor greeted them. "Thank God," he said, spreading his arms wide and trying to fold Ian into an embrace. They'd turned off his electricity. He didn't pay. But he'd thought of how to deal with it: an extension cord was ready in his hand. He would run it through Ian and Elza's window from his window and plug it into their outlet. Not for long. Of course, he would pay them back.

**Elza.** Before New Year's the anti-drug unit knocked our door down. They were searching for the source of a dealer's stash.

The pancakes need electricity above all for making heroin. ("More light, give me more light!"[9])

---

9   A reference to the last words of Johann Wolfgang von Goethe.

# XV
# IN THE REARVIEW MIRROR

Winter sun poured into the room. They sat half-naked at the table, eating sweet Christmas bread. Ian spread it with apricot jam, and from time to time it dripped onto the table. A blob of orange gook glimmered on his large manly thumb with a thick nail. As emphasis. Accent. Accomplishment. Like the point of it all.

**Elza.** Wild horses in the garden. I tensely watch their movements. They're trying to get into the house. Through the windows. I monitor the window handles. But I'm not sure which position is open and which is closed. I keep turning them and turning them. The horses are hitting the windows with their glistening nostrils. Their hot breath fogs up the glass. Makes it hard to see through. As I'm looking out the window, I hear the beat of hooves in the kitchen. There on the couch sit Ian, Rebeka, and Elfman. One horse has gotten in through the air vent in the wall. A golden horse. It's completely white. I run toward it. The horse opens its mouth. I plunge my hand inside and pull the toothy halves of the jaw away from each other. This way I rip the horse into two pieces. As if it had exploded.

Meanwhile, the same thing happened to *Seeing People Off* as to the horse.

An explosion. Tatters. Typical Elza, just her style.

A car in front of the house moved. Yp took her hand off the wheel and put it on Kalisto Tanzi's knee. The road ran through her eyes. Like in a rearview mirror.

Elza was awakened by an urgent scratching at the door. Ian was sleeping. Under the apartment door a very small and fast dog slides in unseen.

PING... PING... PINGPING... PINGPINGPING... PING.

PING... PING... PINGPING... PINGPINGPING... PING.